A REALLY GOOD FRIEND

First Edition

Published by The Nazca Plains Corporation
Las Vegas, Nevada
2012

ISBN: 978-1-61098-184-2
E-book: 978-1-61098-185-9

Published by

The Nazca Plains Corporation ®
4640 Paradise Rd, Suite 141
Las Vegas NV 89109-8000

PUBLISHER'S NOTE
A Really Good Friend is a work of fiction created wholly by Bill Smith's imagination. All characters are fictional and any resemblance to any persons living or deceased is purely by accident. No portion of this book reflects any real person or events.

Rope Cover Photo, Ryby
Art Director, Blake Stephens

A REALLY
GOOD FRIEND

First Edition

Bill Smith

CONTENTS

CONTENTS CONTINUED...

CHAPTER 1

INTRODUCTION

"There is nothing more cherished, more valued, more worthwhile than a really good friend." I had read this sage statement as a child back in the first decade of the 21st century and for some reason had never forgotten it. But little did I know my later experiences would prove over and over the solid validity of the simple quotation written by some obscure author many generations ago. Let me explain!

Few people can say they had a really good friend – the friend that is better than any family – and fewer yet can have a bonded relationship with such a friend over a lifetime. Yet I was one of those fortunate few. Clark Romney was better than any brother, wiser than any father, more sharing and compassionate than any saint, and who loved me enough to set me straight when I wandered into fruitless enterprises. He kept me motivated, alert, and hardworking when my natural tendencies led the other way; he taught me what real love is made of; and he led me to a world of prosperity I never knew existed. This tale is about this great friend and all he did for me for the years.

———————

About the time I first read the quotation about friendship above, most of the world's societies had long ago re-instituted slavery. The abolition movements of the 19th and 20th centuries were widely regarded as a dismal failure, both for the hardships it brought for millions of people without economic resources as well as its devastating effect on the world economy with soaring labor costs coupled with chronic unemployment. When Russia quietly legalized full chattel slavery again, it spread like wild-fire around all the other major nations. Within ten years, 20% of the world's population had been enslaved; by 40 years that percentage had climbed to 60%. Within 50 years, personages available to be enslaved (state and municipal prisoners, prisoners of war, the chronically unemployed, chemical addiction cases, orphans, homeless, etc.) were rapidly diminishing and the price of slaves, once very cheap, had climbed according to their scarcity.

During this period of great social change, the tensions and vigor inherent in periods of dramatic upheaval led to a world powered by an entrepreneurship that ensured a dynamic growth in new businesses, construction, and trade. Slavery was, of course, the economic backbone of the new economy in that it guaranteed a huge supply of cheap labor for every need.

But eventually the once endless supply of new slaves from the huge prisons and jails, settlement houses, rehabilitation wards, orphanages, slaver raids, destitute parents selling their children for whatever the market would bring along with piracy and border war prisoners that had fulfilled the demand so well initially began to dry up. Consequently, the price of slaves, once incredibly cheap, steadily rose as the supply decreased. But, at a certain point, the costs of breeding and raising slaves from birth was found to be about the same as the newly enslaved were bringing in at current market prices.

Furthermore, bred slaves required far less training time since those formerly free were often recalcitrant to take up their new duties and resented being made to serve their new owners in a capacity little different than any other piece of owned livestock whereas slaves from birth knew nothing of freedom or a different status in life, viewing themselves as little more than the livestock their masters perceived them to be.

At this point in time, the breeding farms were supplying sufficient new slaves to the markets to meet world needs at a reasonable price with little further training needed in most cases, and, compared to the old newly enslaved personages, with a much more accepting and cooperative attitude toward their ordained fate in life. Consequently, the newly enslaved properties by this time were viewed as a novelty and were generally the result of piracy, kidnaping, or products of the border wars that still took place now and then.

As a result of this, China, the largest economy in the world, Europe, Australia, North and South America, India, other Asian countries, Africa, and the Middle-East made a smooth almost universal transition from captured slaves to bred slaves. Whole industries emerged to handle this supply process – everything from experts hired to select the best possible "broods" and "studs" from the existing slave stock to make sure new slave stock steadily improved in disease resistance, sturdy musculature, pleasant appealing appearance, and sexual attributes; slave nurseries where the products of the breeding farms were raised to marketable maturity at the lowest possible costs; methods of insuring high fertility among the slave stock; and, most important, planning market trends of the next generation when the products would be marketed, i.e., colors, physique sizes, and genders preferred, etc., to determine selectivity factors in who would be bred and when. Most of the developed nations were now filled with thousands and thousands of breeding farms, often housing hundreds of thousands of new properties awaiting their eventual sales to a vast market of peoples from every known nation in the world, every religious belief, and every color.

Racial and religious prejudices were practically unknown since the big social divide now was between the owned and the owners. Slaves, of course were allowed no religion of their own and their skin color and other physiological attributes were attributed to their breeder's designs, not any ethnic origins of their own. The slave owners still maintained certain whims concerning what they purchased, e.g., black hides went in and out of fashion, whether their properties sported lots of body hair or were smooth-skinned varied from year to year, and overall physique and musculature was almost faddish – huge super-muscular slaves at one time; smallish lithe slaves at another time. Some purchasers bought only slaves hugely endowed; others saw such slaves as freakish and preferred slaves with more normal sexual equipment. Currently, blond-haired blue-eyed slaves with 8"+ penises and huge balls and exceptionally handsome were all the rage in the United States; while Europeans were paying big premiums for relatively hairless black slaves prodigiously (almost freakishly) endowed and extremely muscular, cut, and with beautiful faces. The Chinese preferred slaves resembling themselves – blacks and whites never caught on in the slave markets there – although sturdy Oriental males generously endowed and doe-eyed females with large breasts brought a premium in most Chinese slave markets.

In the United States (as well as the United Kingdom and most other world nations), due to the success of these vast and well-established breeding operations, most free persons enjoyed a lifestyle free of menial labor of any type and even had the privilege of fulfilling even the most bizarre sexual fantasies without social censure – all at a most reasonable costs since the price of slaves remained fairly low and certainly affordable. Many citizens, indeed about one out of every 10, now made their living through the sale, trade, breeding, training, and management of the vast slave population. Slaves, just as in olden times, were the commodity that made the economic engine run so effectively. The free persons of the United States was a polyglot of races and religions (which created an "identity crisis" of what exactly an American was); due to its tax structure, American free society had an ever growing disparity between the rich (the slaveholders) and the free poor (who found their livelihood eliminated by slaves); a society with few limits (what in previous times was viewed as hedonistic promiscuity and open unbridled lust was considered a normal part of human nature now); and an almost universal belief that the United States as one of the world leaders would last forever now that it had been dramatically reformulated into a vibrant slave-based society. Such a state of affairs was not exclusive to the United States – almost all large nations now resembled each other in these basic social characteristics.

This story involves that one-tenth of the free population in the United States that now makes their living off of this uniquely defined class of human livestock, i.e., slaves. [In other words, 13 million people involved in making their living off approximately 198,000,000 slaves harbored in the U.S., no longer included in the census since they were property, not people.]

CHAPTER 2

MY FRIEND CLARK'S BIRTHDAY GIFT

It all started when my good friend Clark Romney gave me a birthday present that wasn't easy to ignore: a young, eager, really black boy with a magnificent, almost hairless muscular physique, one of the most interesting faces you've ever seen, pectorals that were all puffy and begged to be kneaded, a penis and set of balls that were more than adequate but certainly not freakish like some studs up for sale, behavior that was nothing short of being cocky to other slaves yet totally subservient, almost obsequious, to his betters, and an attitude that conveyed always that he was totally aware of why and for purpose an owner would buy him. He was only 19 when I got him, fully trained and, unsurprisingly given his looks and age, had been owned by both a master and mistress before he was given to me, both of whom found him most satisfactory both in and out of bed according to the reports, although both of them had bought the boy primarily for the sexual pleasures he could bring them in various forms.

The gifted slave was yet another product of one of the local breeding farms. Consequently, having been a slave since birth, he had no concept of what being "free" meant, no aspirations of being anything but what he was, and his only real goal was to find a good master or mistress who would take good care of him in exchange for unbridled and uncomplaining use of his body for whatever his owner wanted. In that respect, he wasn't much different from millions and millions of other contemporary slaves who had been "bred to purpose," with the exception this one, in my opinion, had turned out rather spectacularly.

When Clark gave him to me, totally nude with only a red birthday sash tied around his freshly oiled torso, I was absolutely overwhelmed. First off, I didn't own any slaves of my own back then (although I had certainly used plenty of my friend's slaves whenever I could arrange it). Second, this slave had obviously been carefully selected around what turned me on the most: black hides, muscular physiques, handsome faces, huge equipment, and boys eager to please their masters. Third, a slave of this quality, young and equipped as he was, would cost real money – certainly more than the typical birthday gift to A Really Good Friend. Fourth, I had no idea how I would pay for his maintenance (food and caging mainly along with body oil, enema kits, butt plugs, tit rings, a nice collar, genital banding, a strong leash, and whatever else would prove essential over the long haul.)

I had no idea Clark had the kind of money such a purchase would represent although he had, of course, a series of very expensive slaves of his own ever since I had known him. But he sold them off periodically, usually at a good profit, so I don't think it cost him much to enjoy them while he had them under his roof. In fact, when I first met Clark, I thought he was a small-scale slave dealer specializing in highly select studs since he never seemed to keep one very long, no matter how appealing the slave was. But Clark always claimed his interest wasn't commercial – he just liked a change of pace from time to time. If he made money in alleviating his boredom, so much the better. He was so casual about it, he convinced me he just liked to trade his boys in frequently and he certainly never had any of the characteristics of the typical slave dealer, i.e., always touting their goods, showing off their stock on hand, and always trying to ferret out yet another cheap buy or another sale of stock with a jacked up price.

But Clark assured me he couldn't resist buying this slave for me the minute he saw him in the holding pens. He said the slave was perfect in view of what he knew about what I liked in slave boys and the price was right. "It would have been criminal to pass this one up, thinking of you at home all by yourself, probably stoking yourself dreaming about a boy just like this," he had laughed in an explanation of his extravagant gift.

Clark was an interesting fellow and the longer I knew him, the more interesting he became. Born into wealth, he never let money stand between him and exactly what he wanted.

CHAPTER 3

CLARK'S SLAVES

His current slave boy was an excellent example. That slave, now around 24, was about as good looking as males get in my opinion. Tobacco brown, he was well muscled, beautifully proportioned, and nicely equipped sexually. Furthermore, he had about one of the most handsome faces I had ever seen, brutally masculine but yet softened with feminine overtones. Born in North Africa with Arab/black bloodlines to free parents, the slave had been kidnaped as a teenager by one of the freelance slaving firms prevalent in that area. The 'catch' had then been whisked to their own slave training facility outside Tripoli for a year of necessarily brutal and intensive training before he was totally broken and fully accepting of his slavery. During that time, he had been taught in all ways to please a master of mistress, no matter how bizarre their wishes, and the realization he would be nothing but somebody's property from now on.

Eventually he had been put up to auction and Clark had bought him at one of the weekly slave sales in Tripoli. Clark them shipped the slave far away to his new owner's home in Miami, Florida where he quickly adjusted to his life as just another piece of property and proved to be totally compliant with any requests from his owner, including being loaned out to me on several occasions where he was used long and hard (with never a murmur of complaint from him no matter how hard I fucked him or how long I had his throat muscles wrapped around my organ as he enthusiastically sucked away with hollowed cheeks). When I had asked him once what he thought about being loaned out to just anybody, he politely responded in a foreign slave's heavily-accented newly-learned English, "It is a privilege to serve the needs of my master's friends," without a trace of resentment or even embarrassment at being given out as a whore at an owner's whim. I could only conclude his slave training had been thorough and permanent.

Clark had, as I mentioned, a long string of slaves serving his fancy over the years I had known him. The first one I remember was a handsome brown boy enslaved by the courts of his home city of Cleveland, Ohio at the age of 18 on an extortion charge. Seems the lad had threatened some local ghetto merchants with arson if they didn't pay him "fire insurance" and, over time, they got tired of it and called his number. He burnt down a business, was promptly arrested, and within days found himself legally a slave for life, the usual sentence for troublesome people likely to repeat a crime who didn't have influential family or friends to intervene for them. The Cleveland courts shipped him off to the state-run training facilities in Columbus for those the courts had newly enslaved.

After months and months of cut rations, sleep deprivation, the constant pain from whips, lashes, and sizzling tasers, and chronically being fucked by big-dicked trainers who enjoyed hearing their trainees squeal and howl from having their sore butts and throats once again invaded by a huge prick, he emerged on the auction block right outside the Columbus training facility a docile, obedient boy with a newly developed musculature fully trained to provide sexual pleasure who brought a very nice profit to the state of Ohio.

Clark happened to be at that state-run auction and took advantage of the opportunity to buy such a handsome, well-trained piece of relatively fresh meat for his bed. What he got was a 6'4" young man with a beautiful smooth hide, a handsome face highlighted by beautiful teeth and unusual blue eyes contrasting with his brown skin, a well-muscled physique, and prodigious sexual organs quickly aroused to full erection with only the slightest stimulation. The Ohio training facility had done an excellent job – gone by this time was any modesty about his constant nakedness, any shame in displaying his sexual organs boldly, any hesitation in doing any conceivable sexual act demanded in the most public of settings, or any resentment at being a branded collared slave for sale to the highest bidder.

Clark said his first slave was totally satisfactory in every way despite his "free" origins and he only sold him when an admirer of his property offered him twice what he had paid for him. Never one to turn down a decent profit, he convinced himself it was time to try out a white slave and sold him that very day. Clark said when his slave was displaying himself to the prospective buyer and the terms of his sales price was being discussed as he posed with his muscled arms gripping the back of his head with his legs spread wide in the classic 'display' position, tears were streaming down the slave's face to his owner's amazement. When he asked the slave why he was "being so emotional about being sold" the slave had replied "I love being your slave, master, and don't want to leave, unless," he caught himself quickly, "that's what the master thinks best." When assured his sale was exactly what his master thought best, the slave got control of himself, stopped the silly display, and paid more attention to thrusting his sex organs and pecs out for optimal display like he had been taught back in his basic slave training.

His next slave was a rugged-looking white boy from Wyoming who he kept in constant restraint for a variety of reasons. Mainly, he liked the looks of it. Secondly, the slave, despite a long training period, had never completely broken to his slavery and he still dared to show his resentment at times, especially if a whip or lash wasn't in his master's hand. This resentment mainly flared up in dark looks or barely audible murmurs when he was being fucked forcefully up his ass or down his throat. He just never seemed, no matter how many beatings or use of the hot irons (widely used in Wyoming slave training centers), to totally accept these aspects of his slavery, although he was fucked quite often by any number of people, not just his owner Clark over the years. Clark admitted that the slave's barely hidden resentment sort of added to the thrill of fucking him and there was something special in forcing sex on a very masculine man who could do nothing but accept what was happening to him, being a slave now. In fact, Clark said he fucked that slave harder and more frequently than any slave he had had before or after, probably because he loved that look of resentment he usually got when he ordered the slave to bend over with this cheeks spread wide for an ass fucking or onto his knees with his mouth wide open for a good throat fucking.

When Clark showed me some photos he had taken of this slave over the period of time he owned him, I voiced my option that I didn't think he was very good looking – I viewed his body as scrawny for a proper slave – and noted his sexual organs were barely even average. Nevertheless, I commended Clark for keeping him totally body shaved at all times to show off what he did have and to denote his slave status, and added my accolades for heavily tit-ringing the slave, tightly genitally banding his sexual package, and fitting him with a high 4" metal collar to constantly remind the slave he was now just property.

Clark's response to my observations was a good hearty laugh.

"First, I agree with you on everything you've said. But, until you've fucked a slave who really resents it but knows he has to cooperate anyway, you don't know what you've missed. I tell you he was one of the best slaves I ever had when it came to delivering real solid enjoyment in bed – even, I admit, when I had to give him a touch of the whip now and then to remind him of his purpose."

Clark had eventually sold this slave off to a dealer when he was offered 180 percent of what he had paid for him – another sizable profit! I had to admit that the way Clark had outfitted the Wyoming slave made him look like the quintessential slave, medium size prick or not!

The third slave Clark owned was entirely different and one Clark admitted he bought just for the fun of it. The slave was a real primitive black straight off of a Jamaican breeding farm who knew no life outside of total slavery. Treated from birth as livestock, that's pretty much the way he acted according to Clark.

"He was so docile and obedient I sometimes thought I had bought a lamb rather than a human. He had no sense of owning anything, even his own body, and viewed masters as necessary for his very existence. As such, he was eager to be bought and would do anything, anything at all, I wanted. Even when I sold him out by the hour to service anyone who could only afford an hour of a slave's use, he viewed that as part of a slave's life and never complained in any way. I kept him collared outside my estate's entrance, usually with a rent sign beside him, and, on most days I had him, he earned more in a week than I had originally paid for him. Talk about a good investment! I was stupid to ever sell him. If I had kept that black piece of flesh, I'll still be making a mint out of him although I imagine his ass would be mighty stretched by now," he laughed, "and his throat would have been chronically sore."

"Does he turn you on?" Clark asked with a smirk as he showed me the set of photos he had taken of that slave.

"Yes, I admit he does. He looks primitive, as you say, and remarkably fresh considering the use you put him to. Yes, I think I would have bought him for an hour or so each day if he were chained like that outside your estate's outside gate. Did the slave attract regulars?"

"Indeed! The old gatehouse slave that booked him said some women rented him almost every single day and some men were even more regular. After a while, he never stayed chained like that outside my gate more than a few minutes every day. He was already scheduled all the rest of the time. That old gatehouse slave could read and write and I had him keep the boy's reservations on a chalkboard in the gatehouse so he could keep it all straight. You know what? That shiny black slave never complained once at all the use he was getting – even fucking the old hags that would rent him out. He just seemed to accept all of that as his due in life."

"Well, why did you ever sell him then, Clark?" I asked.

"A whore house offered me ten times what I had paid for him even after all the use I put him through. I knew he would wear out pretty fast at the rate I had him going, so I sold him the moment I got the offer. I heard later that they got their money's worth, though. He lasted for a good eight years in that whore house getting fucked around the clock or fucking the old crones who had to buy a buck's use if they were ever going to get any pleasure in this world. After that, he was worn out and couldn't get it up anymore, so they sold him off as a kitchen slave for next to nothing. I still see him now and then. He's the main cook for one of my friends and serves the meals himself – still stark naked and still looking about the same except he can't get a hard-on anymore no matter how much you play with him when he's serving you. But he's a damn good cook at least!"

"Has his penis and balls shrunk since he's not used anymore? I've always heard they shrink on you if they aren't used."

"A foolish conjecture in my opinion based on that slave. The last time I saw him he was just as big in those areas as he ever was, flaccid of course, but still very big. Besides, look at all the slaves who are never allowed any sexual outlets at all for control purposes. Every time you look at them, they're all swollen rock hard and dripping year after year – just the opposite of what you're talking about. I've never seen any of them getting any smaller no matter how long they've been kept from relieving themselves."

Clark's fourth slave had been purchased privately from A Really Good Friend who had only owned the property a short time but needed to raise some cash quick. He was a young white boy who had a pretty face and a nice body but certainly wasn't heavily endowed like most of Clark' slaves. Clark' friend had purchased him solely for his bed but it turned out the slave had considerable musical talent with both keyboard and guitar in addition to a lovely tenor voice. The slave had been kidnaped in Greece when he 14 by professional slavers who saw a decent profit in view of his cute looks. Up until then, he was the son of fairly wealthy parents who had lavished musical training on him as well as spoiled him with every material thing imaginable, including a slave boy of his own, a half-Arab half-black boy purchased for him at the local market in Athens, since that famous city, like New York, Rio de Janeiro or London, offers most everything in its huge slave markets.

After years of searching for their disappeared son, the parents had given up, little knowing their son had been sold long ago in Chicago's slave market after being trained thoroughly for his life as a slave in a contracted African training facility which dealt with professional slaver's freshly kidnaped goods

Although the slave could remember his good life in Greece, including having a slave of his own back then, he knew that pampered life was behind him now and, after being branded and all the whips, starvation, and daily fuckings commonplace in his training program, he settled into his own slavery remarkably fast and certainly showed no signs of resentment or rebellion by the time Clark bought him in Chicago. Clark always thought that was because he had had a pleasure slave of his own at one time and understood the expectations masters had of slaves purchased to give them bodily satisfactions. Clark speculated that his new slave's own half-breed property back in Greece had probably been well trained for bed duty and had set a high standard of what pleasure slaves were supposed to do in an appropriate fashion. Therefore, when Clark's new slave had become a slave himself, he already understood what the expectations would be from a master.

In fact, Clark had questioned his new acquisition extensively on what the half-breed Arab slave was like that his parents had bought for him and found out that slave had had two owners prior to his being purchased as a birthday gift. Those two previous owners, both male, had used him heavily as a pleasure slave so he knew every trick in the book of how to please a male long before being given to his new 14-year-old Greek master. In fact, the slave had serviced both of the Greek's parents as well as the 14-year-old son so he was in constant use one way or another. When Clark asked his new purchase what he had thought of having his own slave being used by his mother and father as well, of course, as himself, the slave had shrugged and said such arrangements were common in Greek households that could afford attractive slaves. Indeed, he casually asked Clark when he was going to be shared with Clark's parents, brothers, sisters, etc. Eventually, this fourth slave went the way of the others – sold to a new owner who paid many times more than he had cost Clark and thus, like the others, turned into a huge profit-maker.

Clark was now on his fifth slave, the mulatto beauty I had enjoyed on many an occasion who would probably be traded in before long, knowing Clark's knack for being bored quickly. I could only surmise what he would have on a leash next.

CHAPTER 4

CLARK'S VAST KNOWLEDGE
OF SLAVERY

Over the last year or so, Clark had taken an interest in how slaves were bred, captured, trained, and processed. Every state in the union, as well as developed countries all over the world, had the need for reliable cheap labor, a useful position for social misfits, and a steady source of revenue from slave sales. Consequently, slavery was now universal throughout the world.

Clark's interests had taken him into the wilds of the African bush where slave hunting was routine, to some of the slave training facilities located in Northern Africa, the Caribbean, Indonesia, Oman, Brazil and Mexico, as well as all the extensive breeding and sales facilities scattered throughout the U.S., Europe, Australia and the Middle East.

Clark could regale you with stories of his adventures traveling all over on what he called "leisurely excursions." One quickly learned from him that there seemed to be an endless supply of slaves from sources all over the world, that slaves were being bred and captured in a variety of colors, builds, and physiques to satisfy every taste, that slaves could be well trained in a reasonably short time almost universally no matter where they were located due to the fact training procedures were well established throughout the civilized world to be effective and long lasting, and that the price of slaves would probably go down over time, rather than up, due to the huge outputs from the breeding farms now located all over the world, but so massive in America now that it was the U.S.'s main cash crop both domestically and as an export.

In fact, Clark predicted kidnaped or captured slaves would become a novelty within a decade or two, that novelty adding to their price over the more commonplace bred slave. But he also predicted most buyers in the future would purchase bred slaves who had totally predictable and highly selected physical characteristics, training since birth, and no knowledge or even a concept of freedom of action or thought. I never tired of listening to his tales of exploring all aspects of slavery, including the sides of it most purchasers never saw – the original procedure, the training, and the final processing before being placed on the block for sale.

With his strong interest in the subject and his ample financial resources, Clark had personally traveled extensively all over the world to various slave processing centers. There he witnessed many an example of the thorough training slaves get before being marketed and was happy to share his observations with me as his good friend. I found his tales fascinating, especially since I could never hope to have the resources to take me to such exotic locales.

First, Clark explained, slaves in the processing centers are exercised rigorously to obtain a good muscular physique that most attracts current buyers, be they male or female. Thus, most slaves put on the block are well built with good muscular definition and with their bodies totally debilitated below their eyebrows either through plucking or daily shavings. They are also taught to display themselves well, often being fitted with a genital ring to facilitate this goal, harnessed if it is thought to add to the slave's attractiveness or is necessary to display the slave's sex organs well, almost always collared permanently, and frequently ringed.

Those destined for the pleasure slave market are taught the necessary skills, whether it be taking it up the ass, sucking down a big one, being milked, or swallowing a big load. They usually use each other in this training so they get well acclimated to both passive and active roles that will be demanded of them by future owners. Slaves were taught to cooperate fully in being milked for their output, displaying their holes properly to attract buyers interested in a good fuck slave, demonstrating their sucking skills on a potential purchaser while still chained up in the auction centers, demonstrating their interest in relishing their master's cum, and showing how they can swallow a huge load with no hesitation.

As Clark pointed out, most slaves were kept nude their whole life all over the world, weather allowing, no matter what use they were put to and almost all slaves were heavily collared with either big leather or heavy metal collars that not only reminded them constantly of their slave status but told the world at large they were someone's property.

Clark was particularly interested in the marketing of stud slaves utilized by the huge American, North African and Brazilian breeding operations. The studs fathering the current crops were as varied as the slaves they produced, ranging from brutal looking jet-blacks to sleek browns with a lot of mixed blood in them to blond blue-eyed boys. Currently, however, dark-skinned slaves were all the rage and, consequently, a good number of his excursions had been to Mauritania, Senegal, Namibia, Algeria and other African countries who specialized in the production of black slaves for a huge variety of purposes.

The most preferred studs in current breeding operations were a medium brown, well built, and heavy hung. They sold cheap enough, often being sold in lots of three or four by locals who specialized in breeding stock, and were usually shown off to prospective buyers nude, totally shaven, and fully restrained so there was no fear of them running away or getting lost. Most potential studs were well used to being displayed fully erect since they understood why and for what they were being sold. In answer to my naive inquiries, Clark pointed out that being put to stud frequently didn't bother most of them. They had been brought up to expect nothing else and had seen slave studs in action since they could first remember anything. It was just a normal function of a slave's life if their masters so decided and was certainly an easier life than the mines or construction work no matter how many times they were put to the female stock selected to be impregnated for their owner's profit.

Some stud slaves, of course, were bought for other purposes than just baby-making. Many a mistress sported a special stud at her disposal as did many a master who preferred well hung, well trained, compliance bed partners who knew exactly why they had been bought and exactly what would keep their new mistress or master happy in use of their body. Some, naturally, did both – regularly scheduled to stud for new slave production, they also ended up far from the rutting sheds in the luxurious beds of their owners. They enjoyed the chance to be a pampered pet of a mistress in exchange for whatever their female owner wanted to satisfy her and it was fun to be receiving a good fucking from a master occasionally rather than always having to be the one delivering a full load. Either way, their mistress' or master's soft, sweet smelling bodies were very different from the sweaty muscled wenches they were usually paired with. Such selected studs had to learn new skills, however, to stay in favor. These usually involved considerable oral skills as well as learning to fuck without discharging so owners could be pleasured for hours and hours with no interruption by debilitating orgasms. This was very different from the stud's normal duties where he was expected to shoot a full load into the breeding wench on her hands and knees beneath him in just a matter of minutes and then having the overseer squeeze his balls to make sure he had deposited a full load.

Some slaves with magnificent bodies, extraordinarily handsome features, and exceptionally large equipment were bought just for the pleasure they could provide their owners and rarely, if ever, were actually put to breeding. But even these slaves, when their freshness was a bit tarnished and the novelty was gone, frequently found themselves resold to a genuine breeder. It was a shock for such slaves to suddenly find themselves in the stark drabness of a rutting shed instead of the luxurious boudoirs they had grown used to. But it was almost a relief to just have to fuck swiftly on command with a clear goal of making a baby instead of the endless games of teasing and pleasure seeking demanded in their previous life as a sexual plaything.

Furthermore, being a 'real' stud was prestigious among their slave brethren and, even though they still fucked on demand, it was considerably less humiliating than being a mistress' or master's sex toy. Also, there was something more basic about fucking to make babies than just fucking to titillate a mistress or master.

In either case, they were frequently shown off, especially with their organs fully swollen to full erection. The breeders enjoyed showing off their studs almost as much as the mistresses and masters who bought them as objects of pleasure. At least, once a stud at a breeding farm generally meant you wouldn't be sold off as long as you kept knocking up the wenches on schedule. Being owned as a pleasure slave ran the risk of your owner getting bored of you after a short while and, before you knew it, you were sold off to yet another master or mistress interested in exploring your body. Some studs at the breeding farms had been there for years and were only sold when they were pretty well worn out as a stud. Then, they were sold off for the labor left in their body but with the knowledge their contributions were stocking the slave auctions for years to come.

CHAPTER 5

CLARK'S PROBING QUESTIONS

Clark could go on and on about the intricacies of the slave trade, but eventually he got to the questions I poised based on my experiences with his 'gift' of a few weeks ago – the beautiful black slave that had been 'used' in about all the ways a man's body could be used to extract sensual pleasure. My gift slave was often exhausted from all the use he was put to, but had never failed in responding to my commands, no matter how sore his asshole or chafed his tits by now.

"Isn't it about time you started making some money in the slave business?" Clark asked me rather bluntly. "The real money is going to be in breeding slaves if you've got the capital it takes to get into it. Nobody wants the bother of breaking captured slaves anymore and the exorbitant amount of time and money it takes to train a formerly free slave. Bred slaves have two huge advantages that are apparent to any slaveholder these days: (1) they're being bred to better and better specifications – better looking, better physiques, better sex drives, better disease resistance, better compliance, better sexual equipment – you name it, selectively breeding the best in class is paying off and it's obvious to everyone; and (2) they're trained from birth to be what they are – a property whose purpose is to please their owner – a bred slave has no concept of free will or not being owned by someone – that's so alien to them they can't even imagine such a thing."

"Well, I know they always bring a premium at the marketplace," I agreed.

"The longer good sensible selective breeding goes on as well as it has over the past two generations or so, you're going to see some real beauties on the block consistently – not just once in a while. I see a future where ugly, runty, poorly filled out slaves who can barely get it up will be so rare they'll be a novelty. The norm will be similar to that birthday present I just gave you."

"Well, at least I have a good stud on hand to start with," I replied, waving to my birthday gift kneeling by my side with his eyes lowered to the floor while I ran one hand through his fine, silky hair while my other hand played with a swollen tit, as yet unringed.

"God Almighty, Brent, you're going to have to show more sense than that if you are going to make it in the breeding business," Clark replied sharply. "This black boy is fine for YOUR bed, but it doesn't have what it takes to make a top quality breeder."

"But, Clark, I can't imagine anything better than this slave you gave me as a birthday gift. He's got everything: a nice smooth hide with an even color all over, well-defined muscles everywhere, a really handsome face, a great physique, nicely shaped organs that display themselves well, and he's obviously extremely well trained as a slave. What more could anyone ask for?" I responded quickly as I moved both hands down to my gift's prick and started stroking it until the slave quickly had a full erection. As I did this, my gift slave spread his knees wide and thrust his pelvis out so I had easy access to his sexual organs. "What's wrong with breeding him?"

"Brent, look at what you're stroking as we speak," Clark retorted. "Don't you see the problem?"

"No," I looked perplexed as my slave was now fully aroused and was now his usual 8"x5" dimensions and was even beginning to drip a little.

"If his prick was two or three inches longer and a lot bigger around, all things being equal, would his price be higher or lower in today's market?" Clark queried.

"Higher, I suppose. It seems the bigger the better no matter what they are being bought for anymore," I responded, still not understanding where this conversation was going.

"You think big pricks are just random on slaves or do their sires have something to do with it?" Clark pushed.

I thought for a moment and tried to think of where I had seen fathers and mature sons side by side for comparison. After some reflection, I responded, "Well, I guess like father, like son – at least from the cases where I've actually seem them displayed next to each other. I do know, Clark, that features are passed on from one generation to another with other animals, so I would think the same would be true of our human animals."

"Anything you breed, you want to make sure you get top prices for them, don't you?" Clark asked.

"Well, sure, Clark. I'd be stupid not do."

"Well, why would you breed this boy here when you could be breeding pricks at least 10+ inches and a good six or seven inches around. You yourself just said the bigger pricks bring the best prices, all other things being equal. This boy put to the wenches will most likely produce offspring just like him – easy to look at, compliant, beautiful physique, but with 8" pricks. With a really good stud, you could get all of that plus a hell of a bigger prick to display up on the auction block."

Finally, I understood where Clark was going with this and, using the black slave's prick as an indication of my new understanding, I demonstrated to him with my fingers what a much bigger prick would be like on the slave.

"Just like this slave's, but with a few inches added here and there," I laughed as I roughly stroked the slave until he was bucking in my hand.

"Finally, Brent, you're beginning to understand what I'm getting at," Clark chuckled. "Breeding is a serious business and you have to take all aspects of what you're doing into account if you're going to make any serious money in the enterprise."

"Other than the prick size, anything else wrong with this slave as a breeder," I laughed as I continued to stroke the slave, now biting his lip to keep from cumming in my hand without my permission.

"Yes, Brent. I've give you a hint. If we bleached his hide a beautiful ivory, would he bring more or less on the auction block, taking into account current fashion trends here in the United States?"

I thought long and hard on this one. I personally preferred the jet-black hide of my birthday gift and knew that was one reason Brent had given the slave to me for my birthday. As long as I could remember, I found black hide just a little sexier and more of a turn-on for some unknown reason. But I knew others had their own tastes in slaves' coloration – everything from skin tone to eye color to hair color to hair texture to even how much body hair a slave had. As I thought of what slaves were bringing at the local auctions, I realized light-skinned slaves with light color eyes and light color hair often brought top dollar IF they were well muscled, strikingly handsome in the face, had near perfect physiques, and were oversized below the belt.

"Well, I would guess making him ivory would up his value a bit in an open market, but not for me, you understand. But, for the local buyers at large, I know boys a light tan or dark ivory are bringing top dollar nowadays, especially those with blue or green eyes, smooth unblemished hides, and light colored hair. Those just chalky white don't bring much, let alone those with some blemishes on their hide – look at albinos if you want to see giveaway prices – but a nicely tanned white or a light half-breed seems to be bringing in the highest bids from what I've seen."

"And – my point?" Clark queried.

"I'd be better off with a stud as pretty as this one I'm playing with right now but who was much lighter skinned and heavier hung if I want to start breeding stock that will bring the highest market prices."

"An excellent answer, Brent," Clark laughed. "This slave is fine as your personal pleasure slave – probably the best one in the world for you. You love his color, I know; you adore his good looks – who wouldn't – and you think his prick is just fine in that you mainly will be fucking his ass anyway and just playing with his prick like you are right now. He's a perfect pleasure slave for you or I wouldn't have bought him for you, Brent. But a breeder – no way! Not if you're going into breeding to make money and why else would you bother outside of making a whole new generation of wonderful male concubines for yourself."

The black slave under discussion was so caught up in trying to control his pending ejaculation he could barely assimilate the news it was unlikely he would be allowed to deposit his seed in any wench in the foreseeable future – indeed, if it was like now, he wouldn't even be able to discharge unless under direct order of his master.

"Master, master," the slave risked a verbal utterance without being asked a direct question. "Master, I don't think I can hold it much longer, master," the slave gasped as he again struggled mightily to control his pending orgasm.

"Brent, look at the slave – he's sweating buckets with you stroking him like that. I'm surprised he's held it as long as he has," Clark laughed. "He's a well-trained buck – I'll give him credit for that, at least. Why not let him shoot off? You know I never bothered to taste his output before I gave him to you. Usually I do, but I was in a hurry back at the sales barn and I needed to get you a gift before the day was up. I'd like to see what his balls have stored up, don't you?"

"Well, I haven't tasted him either since I've only had him, what, a good hour now?" I laughed. "Slave, shoot off for your master in this saucer," I said handing the black slave a small silver saucer from the table beside me. Master Clark and I would like to sample your cream."

"Yes, master, thank you, master," the sweating, heaving slave said as he quickly grabbed the shiny saucer and began shooting load after load of hot cum onto the dish with huge gasps and bodily jerks as his prick quivered while his balls emptied. "Here's a nice load of hot cream for you, master, just like you wanted," he gasped, careful to make sure every drop of his output was contained on the saucer. When emptied, he fell to his knees and lifted with both hands the small silver saucer now covered with his hot creamy cum as a slave's offering to his master.

Both Clark and I dipped our fingers in the thick, gooey output and savored the large dollops in our mouths before swallowing.

"Um – not bad," both of us said in unison as first Clark, then myself, lifted the saucer to our lips and took a substantial amount each to swallow down.

"Delicious," Clark announced as I nodded in agreement. "Could I finish it off? It's the freshest I've tasted in quite a while. Thick, tasty, but not overwhelming. Just about right, don't you think, Brent?"

"Go ahead and finish it off, Clark," I offered. "Thanks to you, I can help myself anytime I want from now on," I laughed.

"I bet you have this first thing in the morning from now on," Clark chuckled, "along with dessert, late night snacks, and God knows when else. I bet that poor slave's not going to have to worry about never being able to unload like so many slave nowadays. Let's just hope he appreciates having such a thoughtful master. What about it slave?" Clark added, nudging the kneeling slave with his foot. "You appreciate a master who lets you unload now and then?"

"Yes, Master Clark, yes sir. This slave is most thankful to be allowed to shoot off for his master whenever his master wants," the slave replied tactfully.

"Well, I would think so, slave," Clark looked the slave straight in the eye. "Not too many slaves are as so lucky at being allowed to empty their balls now and then for a lenient master."

"No, Master Clark, this slave is most fortunate to have such a good master as Master Brent," the slave responded as he bowed his head as deep as his thick collar allowed and gazed at the floor in a proper slave attitude.

"Well, I won't be breeding you it seems, slave," I interjected, "but I admit I will probably be milking you now and then, so you won't have to worry about your balls busting, slave."

"Thank you, master," the black slave said quietly, his eyes fixed to the ground, not sure if he should respond or not.

"Since we've both tasted him now, don't you think it's time you gave your new gift a name?" Clark suggested with a twinkle in his eye, "or were you just going to call him 'slave'? Not too original, you know."

"Well, at this point I only have one slave, so I think I'll just keep calling him that until I get another one. I like 'slave' for a name, Clark. It reminds him of exactly what he is at all times."

"As I said, not too original, and I think that thick collar of his reminds him of what he is, let alone his constant nakedness, but 'slave' it is I guess for now." Clark chuckled. Looking at the slave down on the floor, he added, "At least I tried, slave."

"Yes, master," the slave replied, "but 'slave' is a good name if that is what my master wants."

"He's well trained – that's for sure," Clark laughed loudly at the slave's careful response. "And damn tactful as well. If he takes a fuck as well as he does the rest of it, you're in for some mighty good times with your new property, Brent," Clark predicted.

"I hope so, Clark. Isn't that the whole point of a good birthday present," I responded as I roughly grabbed one of the slave's tits and felt it swiftly swell in my hand.

"That's why I gave him to you, Brent. To have some fun in bed – but...." he chuckled, "buy a fresh stud if you're going to get into breeding."

CHAPTER 6

THE BREEDING MARKET POTENTIAL

I followed my friend Clark's advice. He was good enough to go with me when we visited one of the largest slave markets in the region. I had decided to start my entry into the profitable slave breeding business by buying a prime buck and about 12 wenches with proven birthing success. Clark had advised me a good stud would cost around $250,000 to $400,000 if I bought one with lots of years left in him and with all the best characteristics for breeding and each of the wenches would cost around $100,000 to $150,000 if they had only been successfully bred once or twice before I bought them. It would be costly to get into the 'business' – around $2 million minimum including what it would cost to feed and stable them over the years – but, as Clark pointed out, in no more than 18 years I should have at least my first crop of 12 'products' for sale which would bring in as much as

I paid minimum plus an inventory of approximately 216 being readied for the market not counting twins (12 x 18 years). At current prices, those 228 (counting the 12 currently up for sale) would be worth well over $45 million and close to $50 million if at least half of the products were male who brought almost double when auctioned off. A 25-fold increase in 18 years isn't bad by any standards and certainly beat hands down any other investment I might make.

I could see why Clark parted with his latest pleasure slaves so readily when the right buyer came along. Furthermore, Clark pointed out, slaves kept up with inflation despite the ever increasing supply of them from all the breeding operations. This seeming contradiction was explained by the fact that demand grew even faster than supply so investment in human livestock seemed secure over the years. Even now, the lower middle class were beginning to buy old, ugly and usually worn out slaves to do the most menial work in their homes and to simply enjoy the pride they had in owning another human being. Those with more money generally had several slaves in their homes while the upper class sported whole herds of them. It was clear that slaves were a 'growth industry.'

The internet listings of slaves for sale were vast and seemingly literally everything was available if the purchaser was willing to pay the price. But most slaves were still sold at bricks-and-mortar slave markets in that most buyers strongly preferred a 'hands on' experience when buying a human animal. At an actual marketplace, the dealers couldn't hide any imperfections or unusual quirks that prove disappointing in the long run. Besides, it was important to test a slave's reactions prior to purchase: how he responded to tit handling, ball handling, being stroked, having his teeth examined, and seeing for yourself how fast he cummed, what his stud milk tasted like, how thick his cream was, and how much ejaculate he produced given proper stimulation. Finally, the look in a slave's eyes as you performed all these examinations told a potential buyer more than any write-up – was he perky and interested in being bought or was he despondent and embarrassed? Clark insisted on a 'hands-on' experience in slave buying and I was in total agreement.

As the market opened for the day, Clark and I were one of the first to start checking out what was available. Unbeknownst to them, the stud they would end up purchasing was lost in a reverie of recollections as his naked body was chained into a prominent display position and he was once again stroked into a full erection to attract a potential buyer.

THE SLAVE'S RECOLLECTION:
(BY THE STUD UP FOR SALE THAT DAY)

"Shall we plug him?" one of my handlers asked.

"It would help keep him hard," the handler's cohort responded.

Without further discussion, I felt a large black plastic dildo unceremoniously rammed up my ass while I grimaced from the pain of the intrusion and then jerked as it hit my inner organ (prostate).

"Bingo," the handler said as he watched my prick quiver and then ooze a bit of pre-cum as the inner organ stimulation had its desired effect. The handler twisted the huge dildo around a bit until I was leaking copiously and my prick was as hard and swollen as it ever gets. "There, that should make sure he shows well for a while," the handler said as he twisted the cleverly-designed dildo until it was fixed in position and could not be extracted by any movements on my part. "A salesman or customer can still pump it a little to spruce the slave up if he's not showing well, but my guess is he won't need that the way he's leaking cum already."

I hadn't been allowed to have any relief in over a week now. My hands were usually shackled behind my back, at night I was tied to the corners of my bunk by all fours face up, and every time I tried to rub myself up against the cage bars or another nearby slave, a handler was always there with a whip long before I could shoot off. When you're constantly stimulated by your handlers and not allowed to drain your balls ever, the end result is a constant hard-on, a chronic urge to get you own or anybody's hands on your prick, and a mental obsession with getting off any way you can – even to the really degrading acts like rubbing yourself against another slave or even rubbing your stiff prick against the bars of your cage when you think the handlers aren't watching you. So big, black dildo up my butt or not, it didn't take a stimulated inner organ to make me hard and dripping – it seemed that was my normal state of affairs anymore in this place which literally reeked of cum, sweat, frustration, and need at all times. To think some slaves had to be given Viagra or such to get hard! I was hard all the time.

It wasn't always that way with me, though. Back before I was a slave, I jerked off at least once a day if I wasn't fucking some slut on a regular basis. Like most guys, if I drained my balls at least two or three times a week, I wasn't hard all the time and I certainly wasn't thinking about sex all the time like I was since I found myself enslaved. It wasn't just me, though. All of the other slaves – well the young ones at least – being shackled up for display was no different from me. Back in the holding pens, there wasn't a one that wasn't hard almost all the time and most were dripping so hard their thighs always had some dried up cum visible down the front. That flaky dried cum matched the cum on the back of our thighs where the cum oozing out of our assholes left its mark. You see, you can only absorb so much cum up your rectum; certainly no more than one good fucking's worth. After that, the excess pumped into you eventually leaks out your hole and down the back of your thighs. Since we were all fucked a minimum of several times a day since the day we first had been enslaved as part of our standard slave training, feeling wet on the back of your thighs was something you just got used to – sort of like having a sore ass all the time from being fucked so much or a sore jaw from having to swallow the trainer's big pricks over and over. Overstuffed balls, chafed pricks, a sore asshole, body muscles that usually hurt from all the forced exercise to make sure our physiques were all they could be, and jaws that ached from being stretched frequently were all just part and parcel of being a slave it seemed. At least, that was my experience so far in the six months since I had been sentenced and then lodged in one of the slave training centers (Illinois STC #7) located throughout every state in the union by this time.

My 'crime' had been my inability to pay my debts. Since I turned 16, I had worked at a bakery with a decent boss clerking and cleaning up. But a big chain of bakeries using only slave labor forced our small store out of business only months after they arrived in town in that they consistently offered lower prices. I and two other free men like myself got let go while the owner-boss just retired early, giving in to the ways of the corporate world now and having the means to do so at his age.

Try as I might, I couldn't find another job anywhere. I tried everything: applying to the company that had forced the bakery out of business (they used only slave labor now); trying to get into any of the branches of the Armed Forces (the waiting list for enrollment was over three years long as more and more free men couldn't find employment elsewhere); trying to get into a municipal or state job on the roads (they too used only slave labor now, drawn from their prison population after being trained in the state's slave training centers); trying to get hired by a local manufacturer of trucks and motorcycles (all their labor needs were contracted out to a local slave hire company); and, finally in desperation when I really got hungry and my clothes were rags, selling myself to some locals looking for sexual satisfaction without the bother or expense of buying a slave. Even though I 'sold' well to some local single ladies who seemed desperate enough to have most anyone give them some loving and to a few men too poor to buy a slave for their enjoyment, I couldn't get enough business to buy enough food or clothes, let alone pay rent to anyone, to sustain myself. Besides, doing that was a real gamble – at that level you were wide open to disease.

One night, two local merchants 'rented' me to suck them off. When I had finished with them, instead of paying me as they had promised, they trickily hauled me into the local sheriff's office where they knew numerous complaints about my failure to pay my debts had been lodged. I was arrested on the spot for 'indebtedness' – the standard charge for destitute persons like myself unable to pay their creditors.

The very next morning, the county judge asked me to prove how I was going to pay my debts. When I couldn't, he said: "I'm sick of seeing scum like you luring good citizens into hiring you for your services when you haven't even met the basic responsibility of any citizen – paying your debts. It's only a matter of time anyway until you'll be hitting up the city's relief agencies for food and shelter. Those merchants you sucked off last night have slaves readily available for just that right here in this office," pointing to two old naked slaves sweeping the floors nearby who looked so worn out they could hardly stand up, "and the state is not obligated to take care of you unless you give something back, like lifetime bondage."

"I'll go anything to get any job so I can pay my debts," I cried out in desperation. "I want to take care of myself and not be a burden to society," I pleaded. "I've even tried to join the Army."

"And escape your creditors? Too late for that boy," the judge replied calmly. "You had your chance and you blew it. Slavery is designed to answer all the needs of irresponsible young men like yourself."

"But, your honor," I pleaded. "Give me another chance."

"Once you're properly trained, you'll fit right into the slave population. An owner is exactly what you need from now on – someone who will be responsible for you, give you the guidance you need, and where you can be of service to them in exchange for giving you food and shelter. Enough idle talk. You are sentenced to lifetime chattel slavery with immediate shipment to the nearest slave training facility where, upon successful completion of the training, you will be placed up for sale, the proceeds from your purchase price to go to your long patient creditors as well as pay for your upkeep and training. Any family involved here?"

"My father died last year and my mother was enslaved herself for penury three months ago. I have no brothers or sisters, your honor."

"Good! That's makes it simple. Bailiff, strip this slave and then properly collar and manacle him before transporting him to Illinois State Training Facility #7 so he doesn't get any wild thoughts about running. Next case!"

The bailiff was a huge burly black man, a state slave himself, who, with an aide, almost effortlessly hacked off my clothes with a huge knife he had fastened to his belt around his otherwise naked body for just such an occasion, placed a heavy collar around my neck that he produced from a nearby shelf, and jammed it shut with a resounding thunk. It didn't fit well, but I couldn't get it off and it served well enough for him to fasten a leash to, which he also had fastened to his belt.

The judge enjoyed this little ceremony and, upon seeing my unusually large prick (even flaccid) now prominently displayed, let out a low whistle.

"You're one lucky slave. With tackle like that, you'll probably not end up down in some mine or out on some road gang. More likely, you'll end up as a sex slave if you take to your training properly. Pay attention to your trainers, boy, and you could have an easy life for a slave."

I almost puked as he said this and had to struggle to keep the vomit down my throat. I couldn't imagine ending up as a naked slave in one of the notorious slave brothels located in even the smallest towns now or even as some wanton mistress' bed buck as was rapidly becoming fashionable now – even to the point of being paraded around town stark naked on a leash to show the world what she had bought for her pleasure. With tears flowing down my cheeks, I thought of a scene I had seen only last week involving slaves: a middle aged man, obviously wealthy, was leading three naked slaves behind him – an exceptionally handsome young import from Ireland leashed by a huge tit ring installed for just that purpose; another good looking black boy, about 18 years old, leashed by a ring around his very large genitals; and a tall, well-built blonde man imported from the breeding farms of Scandinavia, about 23 or so, leashed by a ring through his nose. All three slaves were very muscular, extremely handsome, were hairless below their necks, and all were extraordinarily endowed. The Irish slave looked totally embarrassed, ashamed, and humiliated – it was obvious he had once been free, while the other two, being bred slaves, had never learned or since experienced shame or humiliation despite being led around town totally naked leashed by either their sex organs or their nose.

According to the judge in charge of my case, these were the "lucky ones." All these "fortunate" slaves were showing hard, all were dripping, and all looked, well – almost exactly like me in their youthfulness, fresh good looks, and especially their huge hard pricks. The visual recollection turned my tears into sobs of despair as I was roughly dragged out of the courtroom by my newly installed collar.

I ended up downstairs right under the judge's chambers where there were a whole series of individual 'holding' cells, each one sized so you couldn't lay down completely, couldn't stand up, and could only rest with your legs pulled up to your chest or in a kneeling position with your privates fully exposed. Each cell has a wire mesh floor that allowed your wastes to drop down into a flushable water tray below, a full length door on one side that allowed the handlers to stuff you into the cage without too much trouble, and bars on all sides wide enough to allow anyone to handle any part of your body at any time. The room itself was damp and cold so you were never warm and frequently shivered, sweating was non-existent except from fear, and touching a body in an adjacent cage was seen as a source of warmth rather than an intrusion into one's body space.

An hour or two after being caged (and in which time five more new slaves had joined us from the courtroom above), a new set of two slaves arrived outside by pen. They were hugely muscular, tightly collared, and had not one blade of hair on their entire body. Even their eyebrows had been removed giving them an other-worldly look. As weird as their heads appeared totally bald, their genitals had been shaved as smooth as any babies. Seeing their full manhood displayed on a baby smooth body seemed strange and made their genitals appear obscenely big. The only relief from total nakedness was their tightly-fitted tall slave collars that forced their heads into a constant upright position and the thick rings fitted through the septum of their noses, making them look almost animalistic but totally controlled.

Their job, it turned out, was to make us look something like them. One by one, those of us just enslaved by the courts were dragged out of our confining cages, fastened to a 'grooming table' and had a permanent collar installed that was tall, heavy, and tight (which forced my head upright just like theirs in that the collar was 4" tall at least), shaved from our necks down so not a hair was left on our bodies including the hair on our scrotums and up our ass cracks, had our head hair cut with a standard 'slave cut' which allowed no more than 1" of hair at any place on the top of our heads, had our faces shaved, our eye lashes placed in a strange electrical curling iron until they were fully shaped, and our teeth polished.

Next, I was first in line to be flipped over a saw horse located directly over an open mesh drain and fastened again whereupon I was given a series of three flushings which completely scoured my insides of any residual shit until I was sparkling clean inside and then felt a pine scented lubricant being shoved up my asshole. I had never had a flushing before and the experience was totally unnerving, if not overwhelming. It wasn't just having the cold plastic nozzle forced up your anal hole (that just felt very weird); it was the feeling of being pumped full of water until you thought you would bust open that left me exhausted and defeated. Somehow, I felt totally violated by this invasion up my asshole. Oh! If only I had known what was ahead of me in that area I would have welcomed it like a spring shower. When I felt the scented lubricant being worked up my butt, my worst fears came to the forefront. Why would they be doing this if they weren't going to… I couldn't even think about it without fear overwhelming me. Yet deep inside I knew being fucked was a slave's fate. An inner voice told me it wasn't IF, but WHEN if I was really a slave now.

"Is he to be ringed now or later?" I heard one of the handler slaves ask another.

"Later," was the reply, which caused even greater consternation. Ringed where? Through my tits, around my genitals, my ear lobes, my nose? Which would hurt most? How long would it take to heal? Do you feel the rings the rest of your life or do you adjust to the point you don't feel them at all? Of course, I had seen slaves around town ringed most anywhere you could put a ring through human flesh but I had never actually talked to a slave to see how it felt or how painful it was to install. To me, somehow, the septum ring in the nose – like our handlers had – seemed to be the most degrading in that you looked like an animal after it was done, but having a tight band around your genitals made you look freakish – after all, after that was done, your manhood stuck out in an unnatural display and you looked like you were inviting people to handle you once you were fitted with that device. And tit rings, especially when you saw slaves leashed by them, would probably be about as painful as it gets when you consider how tender and sensitive most men's tits are, even without constantly being stimulated by some damn rings through them.

I was then moved over to a bench face down with a wide well-padded leather top that seemed to have an adjustable height mechanism and shackle restraints for both my ankles and both wrists located at the bottom of the four legs. When fastened in position by my arms and legs, the two handlers left and almost immediately two new men appeared, both free men judging by their lack of a slave collar or other signs of ownership despite the fact both were totally nude.

At first I didn't recognize the two of them since I hadn't seen them nude before. But then I was overwhelmed with relief. The two young men had worked with me at the bakery before it had closed and had been good friends of mine the whole time we had worked together. After the bakery closed, we had lost contact. I had just assumed they were desperately looking for new employment like myself.

On that score, I was right.

"Jake? Tom? Is that really you?" I asked, beside myself with joy at seeing the familiar faces.

"Yes, it's us all right, boy, but it's Master Jake and Master Tom to you now, slave," one of the men barked back coldly. "You're a slave now and need to learn to show proper respect to free men."

I was speechless.

"Unlike you, slave," Jake said, "we quickly got work at this court's slave processing center as you can see and are valued members of society."

"Yes," Tom added. "You could have worked here yourself if you had any sense and a grain of ambition. They're always looking for freemen with big dicks, and," he snickered, "you sure as hell qualify that way. All new slaves have to be broken in as even the smallest child knows, and the state only uses freemen as trainers in that slaves would go too easy on other slaves to led to effective, lifelong training."

"As you know yourself," Tom continued, "long before you were enslaved, but especially now that your ass is chucked full of grease, every new slave, no matter how old or ugly, gets fucked over and over as part of their basic slave training. Reminds them of their new status and tells them their body isn't theirs anymore. For most new slaves, we just open them up good over the first month or so and let it go at that. But for the good-looking ones that might be marketed as pleasure slaves, we go a lot further than that. We teach them not just to take a big dick up their butt, but what to do with it once it's all the way up them. You're in that category, slaveboy!" Tom laughed. "Hell, with your big dick, you could have been a trainer yourself."

"You mean your job is fucking new slaves?" I asked, incredulous.

A whip slashed across my butt causing me to strain against my shackles as I screamed in pain and surprise.

"Master Tom and Master Jake, stupid. And slaves don't ask questions – they answer them!" Jake said as he again slashed at my butt rather viciously. "I can see you're going to need some serious voice training if they don't clip your vocal chords first. But since you're so damn curious, the answer is yes. As part of the initial processing, we fuck every new slave over and over until their hole is nice and open and they have learned how to take a big one with no problem at all – well, at least, they know enough not to scream and holler anymore when they're being fucked."

"It's a pretty good job once you learn not to shoot off when you're fucking. You've got to make sure you keep the stamina to last all day," Tom said rather proudly.

"Yeah," Jake added. "We're scheduled for 15 solid fuckings a day. That requires you don't shoot off, you make sure the slaves are greased properly before you start fucking them, and, I admit, you have to build up your muscles to peak condition if you're going to be humping all day long."

"That's why we're so muscular, slave," Tom posed briefly. "Takes a real man to fuck all day long, especially with all the squealing and struggling and screaming going on with the brand new ones. Most of the new slaves are virgins and virgins are the worst ones for a lot of screaming and crying at first. You a virgin, slave?"

"No sir, Master Tom," I remembered to respond like they expected to avoid another slash of the whip. "I fucked my girlfriend at least twice a week before... all this," my voice trailed off.

"You stupid asshole, slave," Tom responded even though he knew full well my pre-slave name but obviously wasn't going to use it now that I was a slave. "We're not talking about studding some whore. We're talking about taking it up the ass."

"Oh," was all I could respond.

"Now, slave, are you a virgin or not?" Tom barked at me again as he ran his whip over my butt as a reminder.

"Yes, Master Tom. I'm a virgin," I choked out since I was starting to cry.

"Well, not for long," 'Master' Jake said as he cranked the adjustable table up until my asshole was at the exact height of his long and very thick erect prick. He positioned his dick at my entrance and begins to push forward a bit as his knees forced my legs apart and opened my hole a bit. "I know I'm not hung as heavy as you, slave, but it's still 10 inches of solid meat and it's just as thick as yours, so you're going to feel it, slaveboy."

"More than 'feel it'," Tom added. "Jake's fucks are memorable according to every slave around here that's in training. A lot of them bleed a little initially, but nothing to worry about – just opening you up properly. Every slave expects that at the bare minimum."

With that, Jake rammed his entire length into me with one huge lunge. My eyes bulged out as white hot pain coursed throughout my body and I found myself screaming even though I had vowed I wasn't going to give them the satisfaction of knowing they were getting to me. My body stiffened as much as my restraints would allow, I broke out in a heavy sweat, and my screaming and gasping went on, well beyond my control. When Jake started pumping hard into me, I felt myself getting hard and dripping despite the horrible pain.

"You hit pay dirt with this one," Tom announced as he reached down below the edge of the bench and grasped my swollen prick and balls. "This slave likes it. Look, he's dripping already and you've barely started! This slave's damn lucky. He's got one of those sensitive organs inside him so he's going to like getting fucked regularly once he gets opened up properly and used to it."

I continued screaming in pain but slowly discovered I could alleviate the pain a bit if I relaxed as best I could and used my ass muscles to push back a little as if I were taking a shit. As Jake pumped away, I eventually could stop screaming and just lay there gasping and panting as he tried to drill into me deeper and deeper. I felt a warm substance dripping down my leg and knew I was bleeding since Jake had given no signs of shooting his load into me.

"He's showing a little red," Tom commented referring to my bleeding. "Nothing serious. About what you expect with a virgin the first time around."

"This boy's damn tight. I'll say that for him," Jake panted out. "You about ready to take over? I'm going to shoot if I keep this up much longer."

"Anytime, my friend," Tom answered. "But make him clean you off as I'm going in. He's got to learn just taking it up the butt isn't all that's involved in servicing his betters. Cleaning them up properly afterwards goes with the territory."

With that, Jake pulled out abruptly which led to another round of incredible pain and as Tom pushed in with his prick only slightly smaller than my own, Jake moved to the front of the bench and jerked my head up until my mouth was directly in front of his huge swollen shaft now coated with warm lubricant, traces of my blood, and his own pungent pre-cum.

"Lick that clean, slave, balls and all, and then swallow the whole thing for a final rinse," Jake instructed as he forced my jaws open with his thumbs and held them there in case I got rebellious. "A slave always cleans his user's equipment so it's squeaky clean afterwards."

I couldn't reply of course in that my mouth was forced open, I was choking on what I was licking off his prick, and the pain of Tom's full entry almost paralyzed me in pain.

The two former work colleagues from the bakery traded off in fucking me for the next two hours until they took a rest, had a bite to eat, and moved onto another new slave they had tied to a 'fucking bench' next to me. Apparently, their job was to fuck off and on all day long with one new slave after another. I was kept chained in place the entire time they broke in the slave placed next to me. But that slave passed out after about 40 minutes, so a third slave was brought in and chained onto yet another 'fucking bench." Then a fourth and fifth slave were fucked by the duo until the workday was over. At that point, a huge hard plastic butt plug was placed in all of us being 'broken in' and we were released from the 'fucking benches' and placed in a cage large enough to hold the five of us where some tasteless cold mush made with coarse grain and vegetables for food (a common feed for slaves in that it was cheap, but filling and nutritious) was spooned out into a wooden feeding box attached to one side of the cage near the floor and some fresh water to wash it down was available in a metal trough attached right next to it. None of us were interested in eating anything due to our pain but we were thirsty and crawled one by one over to the trough to slurp up all we could, difficult since we had to be on our hands and knees to reach it, in the fashion of any other animal we all realized. None of us could even move, let alone walk, without considerable pain emanating from our ass. Three of us, myself included, had shot off while being fucked at one point or another – a residual of our 'sensitive' inner organs according to our two trainers.

Both Master Tom and Master Jake had assured all of us that in a few days the soreness would all go away even though we would be fucked again over and over during that time and that any trickles of blood would dry up – both were just normal responses to a good 'breaking-in' session.

"Within a couple of weeks, if we fuck you at least once or twice a day, you're going to find all the soreness is gone, all the bleeding stops for good, and you have hardly any pain at all no matter how big the prick being rammed up your ass. Oh, you'll feel it all right, but you can take it without too much trouble. That's why we're going to keep that big dildo jammed up your butt right in place for the next few weeks all the time we're not actually fucking you or cleaning you out and greasing you up again. In other words, slaves, your butt holes are going to be stretched around the clock until you can take a good fucking like a well-trained slave should."

I had to admit the plastic plug well up inside me didn't hurt too much as long as I didn't move. But the minute I squirmed even a little, let alone tried to change position, the huge plug made its presence felt with a new barrage of pain inside me.

THE STUD'S REVIEW CONTINUES: (AS TOLD BY THE SLAVE UP FOR SALE THAT DAY)

The exact same routine went on for the next three weeks. All of the other slaves caged with me were treated exactly the same and suffered at the same level as far as I could tell. By the end of that period, we were again eating anything available – most often the tasteless slave mush we were forced to eat and drink animal-like with our hands behind us from the feeding box and water trough on our hands and knees. We had long ago lost any modesty or shame at being nude all the time, of showing frequent hard-ons right in front of each other, of eating like animals, or of helping each other find a comfortable position to lie down in the cage despite the huge dildos jammed up us. At night, we often shared our stories when the guards weren't around and we could at least whisper now and then without fear of having our vocal chords clipped.

Their backgrounds were no different than mine. A frantic search for employment once they had lost their jobs or, in desperation, begging for food or offering themselves for sale. Once brought to the attention of the police for one minor crime or another, they, like myself, found themselves sentenced to lifelong slavery and shortly found themselves in the initial stages of their basic slave training by the likes of Jake and Tom. Strangely, we never referred to the fact we were being raped on a regular basis or that we were being 'stretched' to better meet the expectations of some future owner. No one thought it ironic that my former workmates, both a little younger than any of us, were now slave trainers charged with making sure we offered up a good fuck whenever wanted. Instead, we wondered who we would be sold to and what our new owners would expect out of us. Being fucked was a given at this point, since we all realized that was a given for slaves throughout most of the world nowadays.

Then, after exactly 21 days, Tom and Jake told us they were through with us and they were moving on to another batch of new slaves. The butt plugs were pulled out of us so we wouldn't "get too loose" and all five of us were transferred from the local processing center to the court-assigned state slave training facility (STC#7). Already, we were thinking and acting like slaves in that the thought we shouldn't be treated like this never crossed our minds. Nor did we ever think that the trainers didn't have the right to do this to other people. Of course they did. It was their job to properly train us, after all!

In all my time together with Tom and Jake, they never referred to our times working together back at the bakery, never called me by my actual name, and never did anything but coldly and roughly treat me just as they treated the other slaves being trained by them. To them, I was nothing but a piece of meat now who had to be trained to the state's standards or they risked getting fired, no matter how well equipped they were for their job.

As soon as I arrived at STC#7, the first thing I heard was out of the mouths of two slave 'handlers.'

"Do we brand him now?" was the question from the new handlers, now seemingly totally immune to the pain and suffering they imposed on others enslaved just like themselves.

I quickly glanced around as best I could within my restraints to see if they were branded themselves. Sure enough, they were. I could see a big "S" burnt into one slave's butt from my highly restrained position and a similar brand burnt into the left pectoral of the other slave. I assumed both of them now possessed the permanent ownership marks of their slavery on both their butts and pecs so you could see it front or back. The big "S" seemed to be standard for slaves throughout the United States and most of Europe. It stood for "slave" of course and had been used for the past 50+ years on slaves of every race, nationality, ethnic group, and religion. Why would these two escape such a common marking? And, with a shudder, why would I now that I was apparently a full-fledged slave thanks to that local judge, still no doubt busily handing down new sentences of enslavement?

"Yes," came the reply without emotion... "I've already got the brand scrapped clean from the last slave and put it in the brazier so it should be hot enough by now."

"I'll strap him down for the butt burning first since he's already in position. It's good he's completely cleaned out from this morning's flushing. Otherwise, we'd we standing in a pile of shit and piss when we mark him."

"Yo, but strap him down tight, so I can get a clean scar. You know both of us probably wouldn't live through the beating we'd get if we didn't get a clean burn on this one."

With that, the one slave took three more straps and tightly bound me to a rugged old sawhorse so I couldn't move no matter what. The other slave took the hot brand, now glowing a dull red, and, without hesitation, pressed it into the fleshy part of my right butt and held it there while he counted to three.

The room was instantly filled with a sharp sizzle of burning flesh, the acrid smell of meat being grilled, the smoke of sizzling skin being burnt to a crisp, and, finally, the most horrendous scream I have ever heard. I didn't recognize it as coming from a human, let alone from myself. As the most overwhelming pain I had ever experienced hit my brain and exploded in agony, I passed out.

The next thing I knew, I was vaguely aware of being flipped over on the sawhorse and positioned with a number of straps so I couldn't possibly move the upper part of my body. My pectorals bulged out from the unnatural angle my body had been forced into. Again, without comment, the red-hot iron hit my left pec, the stench of burning flesh filled the room, the smoke of fried hide filled my nostrils, and as the pain again became unbelievable, I passed out.

"You never forget being branded," the one slave said to the other as he studied the deep burn in his victim's chest.

"No, you never do," the other slave agreed. "But you sure got a nice clean burn on that boy's pec. I just hope it's as good on his butt."

"It is. Binding them so tight they can't move no matter how much they try to jerk around is the secret to a good marking. I dare say we've escaped being beat to death once again."

"May God help us when we blotch up a new slave with this iron," the first slave said. "It will probably be the last thing we remember in this world."

"Probably," the second slave agreed. "You know, you said you never forget being branded. That's so true. I can remember it today as if it were yesterday. Is it the pain? The fact you know you're marked for life as a property? Or is it you know for sure you're a slave now and always will be?"

"All three, probably. For me, though, it drove home once and for all I was just a piece of property now and was marked so everyone would know it, especially me, and it would always be that way from that point on."

"Yeah, that's about the way I thought too. But it's all true, you know. You are property to be bought and sold, there is nothing you can do about it, and it will never change. Both you and I prove that."

"Yes. Along with about 100 million more, I imagine," the first slave said rather soberly. "You just never forget being marked."

Both slaves' comments were right on, although I wasn't conscious enough to hear them at the time. After that, I never felt like a free man again and looked upon myself as just what I was now – a piece of property. To this day, every time someone rubs the scars of my brand or my hand strays over either of the brand marks, I shudder realizing my body is owned by others now and their will is my command. And I know that will never change any more than the brand will leave my body – once marked, you're a slave forever.

It took a full week before the scabs were gone from my new brands, but the two slave handlers had obviously done a good job. My brands stood out crisply and were cleanly burned deep into my flesh so there was no way they could ever be removed. I was well marked now as property.

After that, the training continued around the clock seven days a week for the next five months. During that time, I never ate anything but slave mush and only then when told to, never had a drink of water without a handler's permission, never took a crap or even a leak without someone's permission, never said a word when around free persons unless in response to a command or in answering a direct question, kept my eyes to the ground at all times unless commanded otherwise, never hesitated in displaying my body in any fashion demanded of me, and never flinched when others' hands roamed indiscriminately over even the most private parts of this new property. I was fucked at least two or three times a day by one or another of the trainers during their "breaks," frequently found myself on my knees in front of one trainer or another (even other slaves when commanded) struggling to swallow their organs all the way down my throat as I sucked them off to a satisfying orgasm, learned to take a scourging from a slave whip without screaming or trying to escape, and learned to thank my handlers for fucking me, having me suck them off, bothering to correct me with their whips, and letting me display myself fully aroused for their inspection and play.

Over time, I got used to having the tiny scars of the whips all over my body, having my prick and balls handled until they were chafed, and having total strangers ram their pricks deep inside me. I learned to obey any command given without hesitation and never questioned the motives of my 'betters," as I now thought of anyone not a slave themselves. I accepted the fact I should always wear a collar like a dog, always be naked like any other animal, eat like an animal, and that I had no desires or wishes of my own outside of pleasing a master or mistress. By the time they eventually got around to ringing my tits and banding my genitals so they always protruded out in front of me, it never occurred to me to object in any way so enslaved was I mentally as well as physically. I thought of myself as nothing more than an animal owned by others with the sole purpose of pleasing them.

Due to all the forced exercise and controlled diet, my body was now exceptionally muscular, well defined without a drop of fat, and my shaved hide glistened from the fine coat of oil applied to it each morning. I took pride that I was a real thoroughbred, an animal any owner could take pride in. When I stood in display, I made sure all my muscles showed themselves to best advantage, my chest and pelvis was thrust out to best show all my bodily attributes, and that my posture, aided by my very tall collar, was proud and erect at all times.

At the end of six months, I was taken to an auction barn where, each and every day, cattle, goats, mules and slaves were sold to the highest bidder. I was taken to the section reserved for "Studs and Pleasure Slaves" where it was thought I would bring the highest return.

I had a number of potential new masters and mistresses look me over – some more or less superficially, others very thoroughly. Those in between stroked me until I was fully erect, hefted my balls up to judge their weight and content, checked out my teeth, played with my tit rings until they swelled in response, and invariably had me bend over and spread my legs wide so they could insert at least a couple of fingers up my chute to check for tightness and to make sure I was properly trained in taking a good fucking. Those seriously interested asked the auction manager for permission to jerk me off so they could study the volume and viscosity of my cream, and, sometimes, permission to take me to the small lounge where they could fuck me in private to judge my responses for themselves. After the thorough training I had received, all of this seemed routine and I thought little of it, especially since it was happening to all the other slaves up for sale that day. The fact they were strangers didn't bother me – the trainers varied from day to day and hence were strangers themselves and we even had had some women trainers occasionally so mistresses looking us over and testing us out didn't seem unusual. Although I was unprepared for how brazen some of these prospective mistresses were in testing us, e.g., some didn't bother taking us to the 'try-out' lounge to have us fuck them; they just had us fuck them right there in front of everyone.

Although I had visited a couple of slave auctions back when I was free just for the fun of it, I didn't remember slaves actually being "tested" by either men or women, let alone in public. Maybe I was just at a small unsophisticated sales event (very likely), big city standards were less prudish than small town standards, or customs were changing rapidly now that slaves were so available to most everyone. [Later I found out none of this was true – young free boys and girls just out to look the goods over and who didn't have any money to buy slaves were easily spotted and shunted off to the less exciting areas where only the draft slaves and older slaves were being sold off at bargain prices. That way, they didn't get in the way of the sophisticated serious buyers who were hardly at the auctions to amuse the free young boys and girls just out looking for a cheap thrill! I remember how daring and grown-up I thought it was at the time to grasp a draft slave's big organ and pump it until it was good and hard. A girl not much older than myself was doing the same thing to another big old black stud and was practically beside herself with excitement.]

While I was thinking about my childhood adventure at the slave market, two men had stopped to look me over. After checking my body out rather carefully, the younger one of the two began stroking me to a full erection while the older one hefted my balls and squeezed them tightly. When I was hard and dripping, they ordered me to spread my legs and bend over to check my hole. First one and then the other inserted some fingers and finger fucked my ass for a while noting how I reacted to this type of stimulation and made note of the fact I maintained my erection while they were probing my ass hole. Then the older one ordered me back to a full standing position with my legs wide apart in that he wanted to "milk" me. I hadn't had this done, fortunately, since some hours before when a buyer showed some interest in me but then moved on. Besides, all the stimulation I had endured since then practically insured a full load if the master knew what he was doing in milking me.

Indeed he did, and within a minute or so, I was pumping out spurt after spurt of thick hot cum into the small disposable paper cups provided for just such sampling of slaves' outputs. As soon as I had finished, they noted I was sweating, flushed, and panting a bit – all good signs for a stud they said. They each dipped a finger in my cum, felt its texture between their fingers, and commented to each other on how thick it was. The older one, obviously more experienced in checking out slaves, stuck his finger in the cup and then inserted it into his mouth, rolling it around a bit in his mouth before commenting.

"Fresh tasting – salty, but not sour. Very smooth, but not clumpy." Looking into the cup, he added, "and lots of it considering I'm sure we're not the first to milk this slave today. Take a taste for yourself, Brent."

The other man took up the invitation and actually took the cup and drank down a fair amount after swirling it around in his mouth a bit first.

"Tasty!" he announced. "But's what's it's hit record?" he added, looking at my history recorded on a small placard located on the stand beside me.

The older man looked over the placard's contents quickly and announced. "The boy hasn't been bred yet – at least not enough to establish any history in that area. But he's just the right age for breeding and certainly has the equipment for it. He excites easily and his cream is rich and thick and looks as good as any stud's in any of the major breeding houses. Most importantly, his viable sperm count is high according to the lab tests reported here. I wouldn't worry much about him being able to successfully plant all those slave pups we want in the wench's bellies reliably. But more important, Brent, at this point, is what traits are in this delicious cream," he said as he dripped another finger in the small paper cup and swallowed down another big dollop. "Perfect physique, good muscular structure – just look at those neck muscles on him under that collar – nice thin waist and hips despite that massive chest. Unusually handsome face, smooth skinned, bright blue eyes that practically flash at you, curly thick eyelashes, high cheekbones, good head hair, little body hair as you can tell by the lack of stubble on him, even down here above his prick. Nice eyebrows and those tits of his were obviously big ones even before he was ringed. His butt is nice and muscular – very tight above those powerful thighs – and naturally rounded despite all the muscle. The feet and hands are well shaped and not too large. His friskiness tells us he has no joint problems. But, best of all, look at the size of that monster between his legs – neatly trimmed (circumcised) like you often see among most slaves nowadays, well-shaped despite its huge size, and admire those balls that are perfectly shaped and big enough to match his prick as well as carry the big loads we're both snacking on now. A stud's got to have the equipment to deliver his goods, of course, but more important, unusually big pricks are in demand now and mean a good 50% more on any handsome slave's price. You don't stretch a boy to get a big prick like that – it's all in their genes and this boy comes by his naturally. I bet his sire was hung just like that."

Reaching down and stroking the object under discussion back to a full erection, the older man called Clark added, "At least 12 inches here," he said spreading his fingers in measurement along the length of my huge shaft, "maybe 13 on a good day." Taking his hand and reaching around my shaft, he noted how far he was from being able to close his hand clear around it. "I'd say a good 6-1/2 inches in circumference. Anything fucked by that is going to know it for a good long while," he chuckled. "But it's not so freakish he's no good as a stud. Any bigger by much and a wench couldn't take it without getting torn up in the process. No, this is about as big as a stud can get and still function properly when put to a wench."

"God, can you imagine taking that up your backside," the younger one, named Brent, asked rhetorically.

"It would be memorable all right," the man named Clark laughed. "You'd probably bleed for a week."

"Slave, you ever fuck a man's butt?" Clark asked me, the one under inspection.

I blushed and nodded affirmatively.

"Tell us about it," Clark commanded.

"At the training center, they had me fuck another slave who was mouthing off to his trainer, Master."

"And?" Clark squeezed my swollen shaft hard.

"The slave was just reaching his manhood, master, and had never been fucked at all, master. Besides, he was very small even for his age. He.... I'm afraid he...." I looked at the floor despite the hand firmly around my huge dick.

"Go on, slave," Clark demanded harshly. "I'll not tolerate an uppity slave who doesn't promptly answer his master."

"He died while I was fucking him, master. They said he had a stroke or something, master."

"Well, Brent. There you are. Your apprehensions were right on. If you buy this boy, you're going to have to be careful who you put him to and make sure he's caged so he can't get at your other slaveboys."

"I'm sorry, master," I said genuinely to the two masters.

"There's no harm in a slave obeying an order put to him by a master," Clark replied airily misinterpreting why I was sorry. "Besides, the boy's death probably served as a good example to other slaves thinking of getting cheeky with their betters."

"Maybe getting fucked like that didn't have anything to do with his death," Brent interjected. "As the slave said, someone thought he had a stroke. Fate can be tricky that way."

"Look at this thing in my hand and tell me again a puny little punk of a slave didn't have a stroke from having this thing rammed up his butt. If he was that puny, he wouldn't have brought much at auction anyway, especially if he had a smart mouth on him. I bet that was the last time any slave in that training facility mouthed off to one of the trainers, aren't I right, slave?"

"Yes, master. No one ever said anything to a trainer after that, master, no matter what was asked of them, master," I responded almost in a whisper.

"I'm sure the training facilities have to absorb a few losses now and then just to make sure the whole training process goes smoothly. It's worth the loss just to let the slaves know where they stand in society. Slaves need to be reminded of that every now and then, Brent, even after they are presumably fully trained. All slaves backslide a little over time if you don't take some remedial action now and then."

"Yes, even the best training centers give instructions on keeping the training intact in the slave. That part of it seems self-evident to me, Clark. All animals resort back to their wild state if you don't keep a whip right on them. Especially those, like this boy, who weren't born into it."

"Exactly. If you take this boy into your stable as a stud, I suggest you schedule regular floggings over and above punishment beatings to keep his mind right on it as well as make his food dependent on his output. Nothing like deep hunger and a bleeding back to keep a slave eager to please his master, Brent. For example, every slave I've ever had misses the next three meals if he doesn't please me in every way in bed; six meals and no water if I see one hint of defiance or resentment."

"One stud farm I visited required a stud to service three wenches to 'earn' their next meal. Those boys were hungry all the time but they fucked up a storm. The manager said it was the perfect balance between good discipline and starving them to the point where it hurt his investment."

"Well, everyone has their own system. Just as long as it works. Too much whip and you tear up their pretty body. Too many missed meals and they start to lose their steam. Too much hard work and you wear them out early in life. It's all a matter of balance," Clark counseled. "You remember that handsome slaveboy from Wyoming I kept in restraints all the time – the one that resented being fucked so much. Well, he took to getting fucked when I cut his rations in half and told him he wouldn't get back to full rations until he begged you to fuck him to start with, thanked you when you were through with him, and was mighty lively trying to please you while you were fucking him. After a few days of going hungry, you never saw such a change in attitude. Turned out to be one of the best fucks I ever owned. I still kept him in restraint just because I liked the looks of it and felt he benefitted from the reminder of who controlled his life now over and above regulating his food intake."

"I don't think you're going to do much better than this boy," Clark counseled as he again started stroking me. "That is, if you can get him for a half-way decent price."

"Thanks for the advice. I had already decided to bid on him, but that just confirms it.

Now, how high should I go in bidding?"

"I wouldn't pay a penny over $358,000. He's about as good as they get, he's young enough to stud for decades if you want, and he's pretty enough to take to your bed anytime you get horny. But prices are going down and $344,000 may do it, even for this quality," Clark said.

The younger man, Brent, bought me after some heated bidding once I was on the block again sporting a huge hard on visible to all since I had thrust out my genitals as far as I could as the auctioneer told me to. I sold for $342,000 so I suspect my new owner thought he had obtained a real bargain.

My new owner and his friend Clark picked me up shortly after I was sold out of the holding pens just to the right of the auction block, reserved for goods sold. After they had leashed me by the collar, I was led to his friend's Mercedes limousine complete with a slave driver and a slave doorman – both very good looking, matched in height, build and color, both nude, both body shaved, and both heavy hung. My new master led me by my leash to the floor of the back seat where I was commanded to kneel with my knees spread wide and my head bowed. Like the chauffeur and doorman, I was stark naked. The populace was totally acclimated to slaves' public nudity of course but the striking masculine beauty of the chauffeur and the doorman, both totally body shaved to display well, and their unusually large genitalia in semi-erection drew admiring stares and some catcalls from the admiring crowd surrounding the expensive car. Some in the small crowd had admiring comments about the new slave purchased focusing specifically on his handsome good looks and his huge sexual organs. Most assumed the purchase would be serving as the two men's pleasure slave or was headed for some brothel the slave's new owner operated. Such commentary caused the two men to laugh as they patted my head as a symbol of their ownership, but I too was well aware of their stares and bawdy comments before the car pulled away.

During the hour ride to my new owner's estate, I was ordered to suck first my master off followed by a sucking of his friend. Just as I was cleaning my master's friend's shaft off after he had shot a huge load down my throat, we arrived at my new owner's estate and my master and his friend took me to a small stall with clean straw in a large nondescript outbuilding located in back of the estate itself. Nearby about a dozen female slaves were chained to the walls of other stalls in that same building. Looking around, I seemed to be the only male slave there.

"We'll start you with these wenches here," my master said nodding to the nearby females. "I own them and want to get them all knocked up as soon as possible so you're going to be kept mighty busy until that occurs. After that, a lot of slave owners holding female wenches needing to be bred will bring them over and we'll keep them here in the rutting shed until you've done what you're supposed to with them. I don't get paid for your service until they are guaranteed knocked up so I'll want that done as soon as possible in order to make some money out of you. Then I'm also going to offer a delivery service where I'll put you in my slave transport van and deliver you to anyone needing a stud's services. Most of the time, I'll bring you back the same day if we get this timed right – if not, you'll stay wherever I take you until the broods are knocked up. In between, you're too good looking to not fuck you whenever I get the time, including use by my friend here, so you can count on getting your ass opened up on a regular basis. You'll not just be fucking, but getting fucked as well," he laughed. "That will remind you what it's like to be on the receiving end," he chuckled as he reached down and began stroking me to a full erection. "And if I can find anyone interested in using you for their own pleasure, you can count on that too. Doesn't matter whether it's a woman or a man wanting you for their pleasure. I assume your training covered that too, didn't it?"

"Yes, master," I responded humbly as I shuddered a bit from his handling as well as his prognosis of my future.

"Well, now that you're good and hard," my master said as he continued stroking me, "we might as well get started. You should be able to service at least one of these wenches I've got, despite all that milking and such you got back at the auction, before we call it a day."

With that, I was led by my leash to the closest stall holding a female slave chained within it and was chained to the wall of that cell myself by my neck collar.

The female slave knew exactly why I was there, and not wanting to be whipped, lay down in the straw and spread her legs invitingly for the new stud.

"Not that way, wench. On your hands and knees so the stud can enter you properly like any other animal."

"Exactly, Brent," Clark said reassuringly. "Slaves always take better when they're fucked doggie-style. The big breeders have done a lot of research on it over the past few years. Fucking face-to-face may be alright for you and me, but it's not good for slave reproduction. First off, face-to-face is too familiar for slaves; secondly, you can hump deeper they say if your ramming it in from the back; thirdly, all other animals fuck doggie-style and slaves are no different than any other animal. No sense getting them thinking they're any different than any other animal, especially when it comes to breeding new slaves."

Obviously, neither I nor my selected mate had any input into any of this. So she promptly got on her hands and knees with her legs splayed as far apart as possible while I climbed onto her back and, using my left hand, quickly found her vagina and slowly shoved my prick all the way into her despite her moans and whimpers and then begin humping her. I started gently but quickly built up to the deep pistoning expected of a good well-trained stud as the wench beneath me groaned and quivered in response to the deep penetration my huge organ assured. Within three minutes I delivered a huge load into her, jerking and gasping as I did so, my body wet with sweat. She too was wet all over by now and her small convulsions told me she was orgasming herself in coordination with my own. As I pumped the huge load into her, I knew somehow she was ripe for my seed and I probably wouldn't be seeing her for at least 11 months or so.

I was right much to the delight of my new owner who just assumed one session with me would assure a new slave pup was on the way. A missed period the next two months confirmed the wench was knocked up successfully and I would not see her again until it was time for another breeding. For me, there was no waiting time involved. The very next day, I was moved on to the next three wenches where the time of their last period indicted it was an optimal time to be bred. I would be put to them at one time or another that day, spaced out enough so I could deliver a good load of rich thick cum each and every time.

Usually it was in the rutting shed like now. Sometimes, I was rented out and after a bumpy ride in the slave transport van, it was in someone else's rutting shed or in the slave quarters of someone else' estate or even in those people's formal dining room after the dishes had been cleared (when the master or mistress desired to view the mating, often with many of their guests watching also). Sometimes it was on my own owner's dining room table as an after-dinner amusement. Sometimes I was studded with some wench out by the pool while drinks were being served to my master's guests that day. Sometimes I found myself being fucked by some acquaintance of my master or, more often, by either my master or his friend Clark who had taken a special likeness to what my body had to offer. But everyday I was used on a most regular basis, usually yielding three or four big loads each and every day in one receptacle or another. By the end of a year, I had sired over 300 healthy slave pups (as they were called) or 'pups in the making', including six sets of twins. If I could have been knocked up by all the fucking I got, I figured another 100 slave pups would have been produced by all the cum rammed up my ass.

I was a long way from my stupid little job at the bakery. At the rate I was going, I would sire 6000 slave pups before I probably was sold off as a common labor slave, my talent as a stud probably worn out by then. Despite what I had cost my master, it costs him very little for each slave pup I produced, a real bargain considering that I had all the characteristics breeders liked for their studs to pass on to the next generation of slaves. In that same time, at the present rate, I would have been fucked 2000 times at an even cheaper cost even if I had never studded at all during that time and even if I was worthless as a labor slave after 20 years. The truth was, I would be worth about $60,000 as a labor slave at 40 years of age even if I couldn't get it up anymore and every time I was entertaining someone in bed (not studding) was essentially free since my main purpose was to stud.

I could see where slavery was a damn profitable business.

CHAPTER 7

THE STUD'S NEW HOME

"I hope 'Slave' doesn't get jealous of my new purchase," I commented to my friend Clark as the two of us were whiling away a Sunday afternoon taking turns fucking the new stud I had bought. At the time, I was watching Clark amuse himself with the well-built boy we had purchased just three weeks ago and who had 'proved' himself by impregnating 11 of my 12 breeding wenches already from all indications of the tell-tale scent of their urine.

Clark was plowing into the boy's asschute with everything he had, the stud beneath him moaning, gasping and twisting as Clark's eight inches was all the way up him and, from the look on the boy's face, was now tickling his prostate. Clark had the stud on his back with his legs wrapped around Clark's thrashing body so he could study the handsome slave's face as he was fucked by his owner's friend. Forbidden to close his eyes while being fucked face up, the stud's eyes revealed the resignation of a well-trained slave, the excitement of having his prostate stimulated, the pain of having his asschute stretched to the limit, the anxiety always present as a slave struggled to meet the expectations of his master, and the pleasure of another orgasm building within him. There was, however, no resentment in being fucked – as a slave, it never occurred to him that he had any right to resent being used to bring pleasure to his master and his friend. Wasn't that what slaves did?

His hairless body was wet with sweat making his muscles gleam in the dull glow of the afternoon's sun drifting through the windows of his master's bedroom. He felt the slick lubricant so plentifully shoved up him after being given a series of flushings in preparation for this afternoon now oozing out around the pistoning shaft within him and dribbling down onto his thighs as well as the sheet beneath him. But the strong smell wasn't just melting lubricant and sweat – it was also the smell of his master's cum pumped into him twice already this afternoon before being handled over to the friend who was now about ready to add his own contribution up his ass. The slave knew the afternoon would be a long one – probably another round with his master and certainly his friend wouldn't be satisfied with just one emptying into him. If it was like the last time he had been called to his master's bedroom, his ass would be so sore he could hardly walk before they were through with him and his tits would be swollen for a good week or so if they sucked and kneaded them like before. None of that affected his studding, however, which undoubtedly would resume starting early the next day when he was to be taken to a nearby farm where his job was to knock up 15 more wenches owned by someone his master was renting him to for the coming week.

"Oh, 'Slave' as... you call... him," Clark panted as he pumped vigorously into the body beneath him, "is... probably... enjoying the... break," Clark gasped, finding it difficult to fuck and talk at the same time. "This... stud... is... good and tight," he sputtered out. "Of course.... he isn't fucked himself that... often... I suppose..."

"Well, not nearly as much as that slave you gave me as a gift," I answered. "In fact, this is the first time I've fucked the new stud since you came over last Sunday and we both opened him up a bit," I laughed as I thought back how well we did open the slave up then – three times up his ass for me and twice down his throat all the way; the exact same for Clark's usage; and then both of us sucking on his tits and squeezing his balls until he literally exploded with a huge load of spunk that was so good we both ate it completely up for supper before jerking him off again for a second helping.

My gift slave I had never bothered to name was hardly neglected, however. Each morning he emptied my balls down his throat when I first awoke with my usual early morning erection. While he was digesting that, he fixed my breakfast and delivered it to my bed, including a sparkling crystal cup totally empty. After setting the breakfast down on the nearby stand, the well-built black slave assumed a full display position with his organs thrust into my hands and broke stance only to pick up the empty cup. I then pumped him to a full discharge whereupon, amidst his panting and gasping, he managed to place the sparkling cup so every drop of his discharge was captured for my breakfast drink alongside the freshly baked roll and pomegranate juice, which I also favored. The steamy hot fresh cum was delicious after a slug of the icy-cold pomegranate juice and as a tasty topping for the warm roll. Each morning, he never forgot to humbly thank me for 'milking' him as slaves typically referred to being masturbated for their owner's pleasure.

After a leisurely breakfast, I usually fucked the gift slave, still standing in attendance beside my bed, before getting up for my bath and dressing for the day. Each morning I tried to vary just how I fucked the handsome black: on his back with his legs up; on his back with his legs spread wide; on all fours with his knees wide apart; lying down on his stomach with his legs splayed apart as wide as possible; on his knees with his shoulders and face pressed to the ground; on his side with his hole open as much as possible; standing up but bent over with his hands on his knees for support, etc. No matter how he was fucked he knew to grip and then pump his ass muscles around my prick when I was shooting into him for my added pleasure; to 'milk' my prick with his ass muscles whenever I wasn't pumping him but was inserted well into him; and to always look interested and pleased when I had him on his back and could study his face. He knew I enjoyed hearing his little moans and groans as he adjusted to the invasion of his hole by my shaft and his little gasps of pleasure when I rammed into his inner organ. But he also knew I wouldn't tolerate any screams, shouts of pain, or any signs of resistance no matter what I was shoving up his ass or down his throat – even the biggest dildos or butt plugs had to be accepted – even treasured. Although he knew he couldn't talk unless ordered to do so, he also knew this ban did not include thanking me for his use, no matter how or when or how much I or anyone I designated used him.

I glanced over to Clark just as he arched his back; his ass cheeks slammed together, and inserted himself totally into the stud slave beneath him and then bucked and quivered as his first load of the day was delivered well up into the slave's rectum to join the two loads I had already deposited there. After six or seven final thrusts, Clark let out a sigh of relief and began working his large prick out of the stud's still quivering asshole who was whimpering from the ordeal. When he was completely out, the stud, without being told, promptly went down on the cum-coated shaft of his user and suckled him completely clean, swallowing the residue of sweat, cum, and scented ass lubricant with a smacking of his lips before uttering the expected "Thank you, master," slaves humbly voiced after being used like this.

"White-skinned slaves always look so clean when they're properly body shaved like this one," Clark commented as he smacked the stud's butt in dismissal, noting the smudge of cum he got on his hand as he did so, promptly rubbing it off in the slave's hair. You don't see too many white studs hung like this one," he added as he gripped the huge swollen shaft of the slave and began pumping it a bit.

"Or black one's either," I laughed, knowing full well, all things being equal, white slaves were just as big as black slaves until you ran into one group or another specially bred for big pricks.

"With all the careful breeding going on now, it won't be too long until all slaves are as big-dicked as this slave, no matter what color their hide," Clark agreed, stroking the slave he had just fucked until the slave was dripping in need, not having been allowed to empty his own balls in this long afternoon of constant stimulation.

"You going to use the slave now?" Clark queried, moving his hand off of the slave's prick before it exploded in his hand.

"Nope. Tomorrow he's back in the saddle pumping his load out for my profit. But I do have a surprise for you, Clark. Tonight, I've invited a few friends over for supper. You know most of them, I think, so I hope you can join us. Nothing fancy – just some plain, simple food. But I was having this stud and my gift slave serve as the waiters with a little surprise entertainment you might enjoy."

"Yes?" Clark motioned for me to get to the point before committing himself for the evening.

"I'm going to let this stud fuck my new gift slave to amuse us," I revealed. "I won't let him shoot off, of course – he has to save his spunk for the wenches he'll be put to tomorrow – but he can have the pleasure of fucking a very nice looking, tight assed, black boy – something he won't get to do too much under my ownership, I'll wager."

"Brent, you'll ruin your black boy putting this stud to him," Clark exclaimed. "He's way too big for that black to take, no matter what training he's had before he was sold off."

"Well, that's part of the excitement, isn't it, Clark," I replied. "I'm betting he can take him. You want to place a small wager he can't?"

"This white stud's already told you he's killed a slave with that monster of his," Clark retorted. "Now you want to kill off your birthday present who wasn't cheap, I might add," Clark almost shouted. "Talk about a waste of expensive slave flesh," he added disgustedly. "See if I buy any more slaves for you, Brent."

"Calm down, Clark. Calm down. I've been stretching the black boy ever since you gave him to me – a bigger dildo up his butt each and every night when I'm through fucking him. He's now able to take a replica of the stud's prick up his butt with nothing more than a lot of moaning and groaning and some delightful little gasps as the pain hits him."

"I'd have to see it to believe it, Brent. If you've stretched him that much, aren't you afraid you're turning him into a sloppy fuck, like those worn out slaves you see in the brothels?"

"Nope. I counteract the stretching with some exercises each and every day designed to keep the ass muscles tight but very flexible. I've tested him out with the dildos over and over. He's tight as the day you gave him to me – yet stretchable enough to take this white stud with no more than some heavy whimpering and cute little gasps."

"We'll see, but if the black up and dies in the demonstration, that's the last damn slave I'm ever giving you," Clark said with conviction. "Still... it will be interesting to see if what you say is even half true."

"I take it you will join us for supper than, Clark?" I smiled. "I knew you couldn't resist my... shall we say... delicious wholesome food?"

"Your dinner menu isn't what's appealing," Clark laughed. "God, the last time I stayed over for supper you served sausages and cooked cabbage, some wormy apples, and a spice cake topped with hot cum sauce we pumped out of the waiters. Weird!"

"The spice cake?" I replied.

"No, stupid, the rest of it. Why apples with cabbage?" Clark retorted. "The spice cake was the only decent part of the meal, especially since the waiters were so good looking."

With that, Clark left to get cleaned up for the evening event. I took the opportunity to fuck the stud one more time before he would have to go back to the slave quarters and clean himself out again before bathing and oiling his body so he would show well that night.

I cleaned up myself for supper, although I was pretty well spent in terms of fucking slaves that night. My friends arrived as scheduled, along with Clark who looked none the worse for wear considering what had gone on just a few hours before, and the light supper of grilled fish, baked beans, and chopped fresh cabbage was served by the two naked, oiled slaves: my new black gift slave and my new white stud slave. Both were young, well-hung, well-muscled, extremely good looking, and, other than the skin color, could have passed for brothers. Both were devoid of any body hair below their collared necks, both were gleaming in oil, and both sported erections throughout the evening, reflecting their good training. Each slave made no objection to the frequent fondling of their bodies as they hovered over the guests, including having their erect pricks stroked, their balls squeezed and weighed, their tits suckled and pinched, their butts stroked and patted, and their holes opened and explored by prying fingers. I only allowed my guests to milk my black slave, however, for their dessert treats in that I wanted the stud slave keep 'eager' for the entertainment to follow. Consequently, my black slave had to satisfy the lot of them, giving up five separate loads in the process whereupon he was barely able to crawl over to the rutting bench I had had placed in front of us for our entertainment. When I had snapped the bench's restraints shut to make sure the slave was correctly positioned for a good fucking, I led my stud over by a leash attached to his neck collar, picked up his erect prick to once again show its huge size off to my guests, and explained to the stud I wanted him to fuck my black slaveboy slowly and thoroughly for our amusement. The black slave, looking up from his tight restraints, gasped as I continued stroking the white's huge organ and began to comprehend every single inch of it was going to go up into his body and stay there while he was fucked without mercy. I admonished the black slave to not disturb my guests with any unseemly screams or shouts while my other slave was fucking him or he would be promptly gagged with a 6" penis gag rammed down his throat and that it would be rude to pass out. I also reminded him, as he continued to stare at the huge organ on my white slave, that he had been dildo-fucked repeatedly to prepare him for just such an occasion and so he was fully stretched to accommodate my white slave no matter what he thought about it right now. "Dildos always look smaller than the real thing," I counseled, "probably because they aren't quivering in need."

With that, I kicked the black's legs apart as far as they would go within his restraints, and, positioning the white slave so all my guests had a good view of him both sideways and to enjoy his butt muscles in action, placed his prick at the black slave's open hole and then slapped the white stud on the butt as a signal he was to start fucking now.

With a very audible groan, the first half of the stud's prick disappeared up the black's hole followed by stifled moans and smothered screams of pain as, inch by inch, the rest of the stud's shaft was rammed all the way up the black. Once in, the stud rested for a moment before starting fucking. It was during that moment, the black, his eyes bulging out and his body totally tensed, groaned loudly despite himself, and we all saw a tiny tinkle of blood oozing out of the black's ass. Not enough to be alarmed about – just enough to know even the well-trained black had reached his limit. The black slave gasped loudly as the white stud began to withdraw slightly to begin his fucking and again we saw a tiny amount of blood on the portion of the white stud's shaft that had been withdrawn. Again, the white stud paused briefly to position himself for the best angle in fucking the helpless slave restrained beneath him. The black slave again groaned, gasped, and then shuddered as the pain of being stretched to the limit overcame him.

Then the actual fucking began. Over and over the white stud plunged full length into the black slave to the hilt and then withdrew halfway over and over and faster and faster amid constant panting, gasping for air, and the sound of skin slapping on skin. The contrast of skin colors made the scene even more erotic and soon sweat was flying off the stud, oozing off the black slave beneath him, and the distinctive scent of rutting animals filled the room.

After a good ten minutes, the white stud pleaded, "Master, I'm going to shoot. Master, I can't hold it much longer."

The master said nothing for the next minute of frantic pumping in and out of the black's asshole, but then, almost casually, said, "Shoot, slave… You've earned it I suppose considering all the use you got this afternoon."

With that, the stud plunged into the black all the way, arched his back, and, quivering as his load was pumped out in surges, collapsed on the black slave's sweat-drenched back until he was completely drained, his huge balls now loose and flabby. The black beneath him never moved, even as the white stud withdrew completely from his hole, his still huge shaft covered in spent grease, cum, body sweat and traces of blood.

"Have the black slave clean you off," I instructed the white stud, who promptly moved in front of the rutting bench so the black would have access to his organ.

But the black slave never moved as we saw more and more residue oozing out of his stretched hole fully exposed on the rutting bench. The white stud reached forward to move the black's face to his spent organ only to have it swing loose out of his hand.

"The black's dead," Clark laughed. "I win the wager."

"What wager?" another guest asked.

"Oh, I wagered Brent the black slave couldn't take a fucking from something as big as this white stud of Brent's. It's obvious he's either dead or passed out"

I moved over to the rutting bench to check the situation out for myself as I pushed the white stud out of the way. Picking up the black slave's head, I felt for a pulse on his neck muscle right above his slave collar and, sure enough, felt it beating.

"He's not dead, Clark. He simply passed out from being fucked so expertly by my new stud. I told you I have stretched him thoroughly with those huge dildos. I'm not paying you anything. See," I reached down and pinched the black slave's tit to get a reaction, "already the slave is rousing himself for another round of getting fucked."

Indeed, the black slave did moan slightly but was unable to open his eyes yet. He had heard, as if he were a great distance away, something about getting fucked again and slipped back into unconsciousness. But he came to again when he felt the shackles being released from his ankles and wrists and felt the white stud lift him off the rutting bench and onto a nearby chair where he slowly came back into this world.

"Thank you, master," seemed to be the only thing to say. Indeed it was. His master, seeing the slave wouldn't be much good to fuck anymore that night ordered the white stud to lift him up over his shoulder and for the two of them to hit the flushing room and then bathe themselves. They were through for the night, he said, and had permission to rest up for tomorrow. Both slaves now quickly said "Thank you, master," and left the room before the command was reversed. But not before they received applause from the dinner guests, including their master's friend Clark.

"Well done, Brent!" they all said in unison. "Most entertaining." Both slaves leaving the room knew their value went up a bit with that accolade, but both also knew fame brought even greater use.

The next morning, the black slave was back into his regular routine, first sucking off his master and then fixing the breakfast, which would lead to producing the usual breakfast snack of hot cum for his master and then probably getting soundly fucked before his master prepared for the day's activities.

That activity would include taking the white stud in his slave transport van to the nearby farm that was renting his stud's service. He felt certain the white stud would have the lot of them knocked up by the end of the week and he'd be pocketing the fairly high stud fees when he picked him up next Saturday, hopefully none the worse for wear. He'd be sure to remind the stud of exactly what was expected of him by that time and to tell the neighbor renting him to keep the stud right at it to get the job done as quickly as possible. Sometimes, even the best studs needed a little reminder on their backsides of just why they had been purchased to start with.

By next Saturday night, my black slave was completely back into his regular routine of servicing all of my needs with enthusiasm and any soreness or bleeding from entertaining my guests had long gone. Since I fucked him at least twice a day during that week, I didn't ascertain that the entertainment had hurt him in any way – he seemed just as tight and receptive as he always had. My exercise program paid off! Even my friend Clark, who fucked him twice on Wednesday during a visit, admitted having the prodigiously equipped white stud fuck him didn't seem to have any lasting effect one way or the other.

I had picked up my white stud as scheduled in that the wenches he had been put to repeatedly were all now probably successfully impregnated with new slave pups going by his past record. Although he was tired and his prick was a little chafed, he wasn't completely tuckered out in that I was able to stroke him to a full erection in only a little more time than usual. His balls were sore, however, from so much use, and he flinched with I squeezed them to test for fullness. They were spongy and soft – that neighbor had completely drained them over the week but then, he had paid his money for just that. I figured with a two-day "re-charging" rest over Sunday and Monday, I could load him up in the slave transport van again on Tuesday morning for a visit to another neighbor seeking his services with his own brood of wenches awaiting impregnation.

CHAPTER 8

BUYING A SECOND STUD
FOR NEXT TO NOTHING

The first year of slave breeding had gone well. The first pups were popping out of the selected wenches right on schedule and the stud-for-rent business was fully booked due to the slave's sure-fire record of 'hits.' We were getting impregnations about half the time now if we put the broods under him at just the right time in their ovulation cycle and didn't over-schedule him so he had plenty of time to manufacture a good fertile load before he was called to duty once again. The sturdy white stud never complained that I heard of and still seemed amiable to getting fucked himself fairly regularly by me and my friends. My best friend Clark had never lost his attraction to the muscular well-hung boy and he alone made sure the boy's ass was kept open and well used.

Meanwhile, I still had my 'gift slave," the handsome jet-black slave given me by Clark. He too had never failed to satisfy, no matter what I demanded of him. In fact, he seemed even more eager to please me than when he had first been gifted to me. I supposed he was getting used to his new owner, to the role of a good pleasure slave in the 21st century, and to the fact he had escaped the horrors of the mines and construction crews as long as he was found pleasing in bed. Like my white stud, he was well fed, well exercised, and protected from the much harsher lives most slaves endured throughout the contemporary world and, again like my white stud, was most appreciative of that.

But, of course, he was a bred slave, who predictably settled into whatever role they were sold into. My preference to shiny jet-black hides hadn't diminished one iota due to the ready availability of just such a package anytime I was in the mood. While other owners seemed to satiate on particular colors or builds with the ready access ownership made possible, the opposite seemed to happen in my case – I practically got addicted to having sex with my black slave and tended to be dissatisfied sexually when using my friend's slaves urged upon me as part of their hospitality or slaves loaned out to me for a trial run by the auction houses. Indeed, even fucking my magnificently built white stud slave didn't have quite the kick in it I found in fucking the gifted black.

After all this time, I still thought my black pleasure slave should be studding so that I could be selling off clones of him in another 15 to 20 years. But Clark's arguments against it prevailed and so my black slave's prick never entered a woman and his sperm was never used for making new slaves. Other than letting him shoot off occasionally while I was fucking him sometimes or, much more often, milking him for a tasty little snack, almost all cum connected with my black pleasure slave was someone else's and was going the other way: either down his throat or up his rectum. The black's cock-sucking skills were even better than they were when I first got him – he could now swallow even the biggest pricks all the way down without gagging or choking and holding it there until he had extracted a full load deep into his stomach. Moreover, his ability to offer up an exquisite fuck was unparalleled – he had trained his ass muscles to actually pump a shaft inserted in him without any effort on the part of the person fucking him and he knew exactly when to clamp down on a deeply inserted penis at just the right time to give the fucker more satisfaction than he had ever experienced before with a slave, no matter how well trained they claimed they were. Despite the fact his penis wasn't the gigantic size of most slaves selected as studs; I still felt he would sell for well over $300,000, even in today's crowded markets.

Five years later, I remained just as enamored with my black slave as I had ever been and still continued to use him several times each and every day. Unlike my friend Clark, I wasn't one to tire easily of a good thing and consequently never copied my friend in his habit of constantly selling off stock for a profit and replacing it with something new and different and then selling that off as he got bored. Clark, as far as I was concerned, was little different than a slave dealer other than he certainly enjoyed his stock on hand at any given time. He made tremendous profits along the way while never suffering from not having some good looking slave around to service him at any given time.

My white stud was still at it with no 'down-time' and my slave nurseries were jammed full of stock rapidly pursuing the destiny which fate had ordained for them though the circumstances of their birth.   In another decade, the eldest among them would be reaching the final stages of their training and a few years after that would be at their peak, proudly displaying themselves, their handsome muscular bodies gleaming with a fresh coat of oil and their pricks in full erection, on an auction block as the bids on them went higher and higher.

But, in the interim, I had a hell of a lot of brood mares to feed, practically an army of pups who ate even more, and some trainers that had to be paid what they were worth.

But Clark didn't have to remind me that I needed a black stud to join my white one. The market forces were clear. Clark had been right years ago in predicting the future market for handsome white slaves. Now, black slaves, for whatever reason, were becoming more and more popular and consequently were selling for more. It was obvious if the trend continued, the price premium once given to white slaves would shift to black slaves. Indeed, in some regions of the country, blacks were already selling about 10% more than whites, all other factors being equal. Blacks hung like horses were especially desirable, even, strangely, where the size of their pricks had nothing to do with their duties once bought. It was easy to see the premium money being spent on black bucks going to the public brothels or to the pleasure slave and stud markets. But why did extraordinarily hung blacks bring more at the auctions when they were headed for the construction crews, the mines, and the manufacturing plants where their big pricks would get little to no use outside of being played with by their overseers and handlers? Public fashions seemed so fickle, especially when it came to slaves and the prices they sold for. Nevertheless, it was obvious I was going to have to find the means, somehow, to come up with a black stud with all the 'best' genetic traits the market demanded. But how?

Clark, as usual, found a solution to my problem. A few months ago, a large freight train included a slave transport railway car, which was delivering a batch of freshly purchased black studs to a very large breeding operation near Birmingham, Alabama. These new purchases, as could be expected, possessed all of the traits desirable in male breeding stock: big, muscular, disease-resistant, strikingly handsome, flawless skin, and, of course, sex organs so big only a handful of slave women could be coupled with them, even opened up by previous pregnancies and well-greased to boot. The carefully selected black studs had sold at astronomical prices, still the talk of the slave market reports.

Upon their sale, they had been herded into 10 slave transport cages holding five slaves each, fully equipped with fresh straw and water bottles clamped on all the open bars making up the sides of the cages, and then close chained into a highly restricted crouching position within one cage of another for the long trip. The close chaining of the slaves kept the owner's investment secure as well, of course, kept them from fucking the other slaves in their particular cart, sucking each other, or even playing with themselves the duration of the trip. They could, however, reach the water nozzle closest to their restrained position. These ten cages were then placed within a standard livestock railroad car widely used for long distance transfer of slaves, cattle, sheep, and horses. All the studs had been cleaned out thoroughly in preparation for the long

train trip and they could piss in place easily enough
– the open air carts allowed good ventilation although
nights would be a little chilly, especially since they
couldn't hunch against each other for warmth as most
had done in the holding pens of the auction house.
With the numerous whips of the loaders cracking over
their naked hides and the occasional sizzle of tasers,
some yelps and screams were inevitable until all these
epitomes of male perfection were in their barred cages,
chained with their hands behind their back and their
legs shackled together, and ready for the long trip.

Four hours later, the journey well underway,
the slave transport car happened to be right beside a
sugar processing plant. Without warning, the plant
burst into a huge spontaneous explosion (an electrical
short circuit had ignited the gases used in sugar
refining) whereupon the slave handlers and all the
precious slave cargo were instantly killed in a cloud
of flaming chemicals, pelting debris and thick clouds
of poisonous gases. Of the 51 stud slaves being taken
to their new home, about half were instantly killed
by the hot iron bars of their cages thrust through
their bodies as the transport cages were twisted and
crushed by the pelting debris. The other half were
burnt to death by the flaming gases, unable to escape
due to their constraining chains and iron cages until
they were just pieces of charred black flesh totally
unrecognizable as human stock anymore. The slave
handlers accompanying the 10 cages, along with a
few other draft slaves brought along for unloading
the cages, were all killed in the first wave of hot ashes,
generally suffocating to death before they were cooked
by the hot gases.

The happy news was that the new owners
of the slaves were fully insured and got back what

they had paid for their new supply of studs. But the slave handlers and the draft slaves accompanying them (belonging to the contracted slave transport company) were not insured – the contacted slave transport company got nothing for their loss. All of the company's slave cages, the three well-trained slaves utilized as handlers owned by the company, along with the three company draft slaves used for the grunt work, had to be written off as a total loss, a considerable set-back even for a company in the slave transport business for a number of years.

Within a week after the accident, a flesh batch of new "equally good" black studs had already been purchased at yet another large market in Detroit, Michigan and had already reached their designated destination near Birmingham, Alabama, where they were getting their first experience at the rutting benches.

What wasn't reported was that one stud in the fiery inferno had actually survived, albeit horribly scarred on his upper body and with a face grotesquely disfigured, so badly people gasped in horror when they viewed him. The damage was confined to the upper part of the slave's body though, so, from the waist down he remained just as magnificent as when he had first been sold as a promising stud. Clark had found out about this survivor from an insurance company agent who was willing to take whatever he could get for the slave at salvage prices. Clark said it was the answer to my prayers.

Upon Clark's insistence, we went to the insurance company slave pens and I almost puked when I first saw this monster. He had one runny eye left, no jaw but a few ragged teeth hanging through what was left of an upper lip, no ears, and no nose but a hole where one might have once been. He could barely see with his one distended eye, couldn't hear anymore with no ears, breathed nosily through the hole that used to be a nose, and could only eat the soft slave mush or liquefied slave gruel with no fixed teeth in place. He could only grunt since his vocal chords were burnt away and his head hung to one side of his slave collar due to his neck tendons being severed as he had struggled to break his restraints in panic.

I quickly diverted my eyes from the sickening sight and turned my back to his cage.

"Brent, don't look at his ugly topside which I admit is about as gross as it gets. But turn around and look at this thing below the waist. Don't look up, just down below the waist and tell me you don't like what you see."

I turned and did as he said; being careful not to look upward at what had once been a human being. What I saw was amazing. Totally unscarred, totally unblemished in any way was a perfect set of abs, well tapered muscular thighs, great calves and feet, a nicely rounded muscular butt, and, spectacularly, the biggest, most perfectly shaped prick and set of balls I had ever seen, including the white stud I owned who I though was about as big as men got. This black had it all over my white stud by a good two inches in length and another inch or two in girth. Even flaccid, he was at least 10"x6". I couldn't imagine him erect.

"Slave, display," Clark ordered sharply with a smack to the slave's butt. The slave, unable to hear the verbal command, understood from the smack what was wanted and thrust out his organs and tensed his butt but was physically unable to put his hands in back of his neck or display his scarred chest in any way.

"Now, Brent, don't look up but take that big prick in your hand and start stroking it. I want you to see for yourself what's left of this boy's body."

Being careful not to look at the slave's flagitious face again, I did as my friend directed and within less than a minute, the huge prick swelled steadily in my hand until it had grown a good three inches in length and a good three more inches around and attempted to stand out from his body, the sheer weight of the huge organ preventing it standing out more than 45 degrees or so from his body. Nevertheless, continued stroking led to a quick dribbling at the end of the huge prick as pre-cum worked its way to the opening. The immense prick quivered in my hand, now unable to hold the huge thing with just one hand. The black's prick alone must have weighed a couple of pounds in and of itself.

"Imagine him wearing a full metal mask, a completely covered head cage, over his face at all times – a full head and face covering welded on forever with only a hole for feeding and another that allowed him to breathe, affixed so as to make sure it held his head upright at all times, and a fitted aluminum plate harness covering the top part of his torso so you never saw those scars from the burning. He can't see or hear anything anyway, so there's no need to look at his ugliness. He can always be led around with a leash we'll attach to this full covered helmet and he'll take all his commands from smacks on the butt. One smack for display; two to fuck; three to stop fucking; four to take a milking; and so on and so forth. He'll learn quickly enough."

I was speechless as I kept stroking the huge thing in my hand until, with a tightening of his hips and a small grunt accompanied with some heavy breathing, the stud deposited a huge load of steaming hot cum into my hand and spilling out onto the concrete floor beneath us.

"The insurance company's claim agent will sell him to you for a mere $3500 if you take him today," Clark continued. "He wants to get the account closed out and the whole matter behind him."

"A covered head cage and an upper body harness like a suite of armor?" I muttered as I tried to wipe some of the cum off of my hand, knowing I couldn't rub it off in the slave's non-existent head hair or have him lick me clean.

"Did you ever see slaves with covered heads, Brent?"

"Well, yes, Clark. Not too long ago I went to a boxing match where the two boxers, slaves of course, had their heads completely covered with some sort of plastic protective helmets along with another plastic device protecting their genitals. I suppose they were good looking boys and their owners didn't want to risk damaging their good looks as well as their ample sexual equipment, especially since both of the slave boxers were being offered as bed bucks for a pretty stiff fee for the night as soon as the fight was over." I chuckled as I recalled one of the boxers was rented out to a rather fat middle age lady; the other boxer was sold for the evening to a stout little man in his fifties.

"I've seen those helmets," Clark responded. "They're made out of some strong, rigid plastic like Teflon or Lexon, I imagine."

Then I told Clark it reminded me of a novel I had read years ago called 'The Man in the Iron Mask' in which a prince was kidnaped by a pretentious usurper and placed in an isolated prison a considerable distance away. The prince's nemeses hid his true identity from the public by having a full covered helmet permanently locked in place on him after severing his vocal chords so he could never reveal who he had once been.

"No different. We'll have one made up and welded on him in no time and an aluminum or Teflon body cast to cover his upper torso will be easy enough to come by. Shouldn't cost you more than $2000 or so at most, including welding it on," Clark said excitedly. "Just think, Brent. For a total of $5500, you're going to have one of the best black studs in the business. What he looks like now has nothing to do with the genes he'll be passing on each and every day. His offspring will look as good as he did before the accident. I have a photo of what he used to look like that the insurance guy gave me – turns out the insurance companies routinely photograph what they are insuring – so you can see for yourself," Clark added as he thrust the insurance company's routine digital photo of a strikingly handsome, even beautiful, totally naked black slave in front of me. "That's him," Clark pointed out. "That's what his pups will look like."

"It's a deal if this full helmet and body harness of yours covers that face and upper body completely and forever," I responded. "I can't stand looking at him like that," I added for good measure.

"Neither could the wenches you'll be putting him to," Clark laughed. "With the covered head cage locked in place, they can only imagine what a handsome man lies behind it. All they'll know for sure is what they're being fucked with so my guess is they'll think a Greek god himself is underneath that metal helmet."

"Are you sure we can get food and water in him with the helmet on?" I queried.

"No problem. You can feed him slave gruel through a thick plastic tube or even a flexible metal pipe – anything he can suck through with what's left of his mouth. Same with the water," Clark assured me. "We'll make sure it will fit right through the helmet's mouth hole."

The very next day, Clark, ever a great friend, had found a metalsmith who made up the helmet and installed it permanently. It was made of a bright bronze for light weight, decorated with touches of silver plate, and featured a relief like that of a Roman god – beautiful high cheekbones, prominent eyebrows (now silver plate), a beautiful Greek nose (which allowed plenty of air to pass through to the hole in his head where a nose had once been), a delicate mouth with silver plated lips (slightly open so the plastic feeding tube would easily fit through it), and a new bronze slave collar with leash rings all around it molded into the bottom of the full helmet to assure it would never come off his thick muscled 20" neck. A plastics specialist shop had made up a Lexon plastic harness that expanded to cover all of his upper body, including his back, shoulders, and pectorals (all the scarred areas), which emphasized his size, build, and yet was flexible enough for him to move around easily. It was a semi-rigid, yet unbreakable plastic, which would last for years, was lightweight, and, since it was fixed in place, could withstand the daily washings the slave would have for cleanliness. The shiny black plastic covering featured huge simulated molded pectorals, prominent nipples, and rippled abdominal muscles that would match the magnificence of the slave's naked body fully exposed below his waist.

When all had been installed, the black slave was magnificent. Masked in splendor above; totally naked, fully shaved, and exposed below where his present prized attributes were located.

"Won't the slave get too hot encapsulated in all that metal and plastic?" I asked, imagining such a device welded on me. "Imagine the sweat under all that bronze."

"He'll get used to it," Clark assured me. "Besides, the metalsmith put a few small vent holes right above where it's welded to his collar and at the top of the helmet. No one can see in, but it lets some air through. And the plastic vest is microscopically perforated with holes so small you can't see them so the skin underneath can breathe. Besides, it's just a slave and you know how they get used to things over time."

"Oh, I didn't notice the vent holes," I replied. "And you're right, Clark. I suppose a slave would get used to that just like they do a collar or the ring around their manhood," I assured myself. "Slaves adjust to about anything."

When I leashed him for the first time and led him back to my breeding barn, I knew my prayers for prosperity had been answered. For a few thousand dollars, hundreds of full black pups could now be added to my growing stock of whites and mulattoes. As Clark forecast, those new black pups would sell for even more than my white ones and no one would know they had been bred by a literal monster.

Everything worked out exactly as Clark had said it would. The helmet and upper body plastic covering never came off the black stud so no one ever saw his horrible disfigurement again. He could be fed easily enough; he could breathe through his new 'nose' and he didn't need to hear or see or talk for what he was purchased to do. He could be led to his duties on a leash and given orders through slaps on his muscular rump. He had no trouble humping on command and delivered a big load each and every time with a hit rate rivaling my white stud who's learned to like his new companion over time even though he couldn't talk, couldn't hear, and couldn't see. But the helmeted black stud liked being fucked by the white occasionally and didn't mind returning the favor when their owner found that amusing.

One night, after I had finished fucking my white stud to my complete satisfaction, the slave risked asking me a question.

"Master, I know slaves aren't supposed to ever talk unless answering a question or acknowledging a command, but I just wonder why your new black stud is covered by his helmet and plastic torso covering all the time?" he quietly asked, knowing he could be severely punished for speaking out like this. "Is he being punished?"

I immediately slapped the white stud across his face for his impertinence, but decided to answer.

"It's so you don't get jealous of him," I answered. "He's so good looking it would make you feel inferior if you could see all of him, not just that huge prick of his."

"Thank you, master," the white stud answered but then decided to risk speaking again despite being slapped previously. "The black stud is about the heaviest hung slaveboy I've ever seen, Master" he giggled. "But, master, I wouldn't be jealous of him – I'm not jealous of your pleasure slave and he's about as good looking as slaves get if seems."

"I can see why, with me letting you fuck him occasionally when my guests need a little entertainment."

"Yes, master," the white stud smiled.

"Just let me make the decisions around here, slave. I note the helmet doesn't keep you from fucking the black stud when you get a chance."

"No, master. Nor him fucking me when master decides," he giggled again.

"You've got me all horny with all this slave talk. Get on your hands and knees, boy, with your legs spread so your hole is open. I'm in the mood to fuck you again."

"Yes, master," the white slave replied as he quickly assumed the commanded position and sighed deeply as I entered him for the second time that night. When I was all the way up him, he muttered "Thank you, master," as I began to plow in and out of his still tight hole.

That was the last time I ever got a question about the black stud's helmet and permanent torso covering. Neither the white stud nor my black pleasure slave ever inquired again about the strange apparition that, over time, became part and parcel of the black stud. But then, slaves don't ask questions of their masters.

CHAPTER 9

THE ESTATE SETTLEMENT

TWO YEARS LATER:

I had just finished giving the eulogy for my close friend Clark. He had died in a tragic auto accident returning, as was so typical of him, from a slave merchant in a city less than 50 miles away who had come across an exceptionally handsome slave recently imported from Syria he had thought would interest Clark. The merchant was right. Clark had bought the beautiful brown 18-year-old on the spot following a thorough body inspection for a very hefty price and, after shackling and placing the new purchase in one of the slave cages permanently fitted into the back of his Cadillac Escalade, had intended to bed the boy down properly once he was back at his estate.

But fate intervened.   In the first hour after departure, Clark was caught in a nine-car pile-up during a severe rainstorm on the interstate and he, along with the caged Syrian slave in the rear compartment, were instantly killed. Ironically, it was the state polices' own slaves that removed the corpses from the crash so even in death, Clark was being tended to by slaves.

My eulogy pointed out Clark's zest for life, his enjoyment of his always rotating stable of handsome slaveboys, his generosity in frequently sharing his slaveboys with his friends, his willingness to share his vast knowledge about almost all aspects of slavery with other slaveholders even to the point of sometimes accompanying a brand new slave purchaser to the market to help them sort out all the goods and to get a decent price, and, finally, how Clark had given me outright my very first slave, a boy I had never tired of and I still had at home.

I emphasized that Clark Romney was born into money and never had the need to engage in a career himself, but this did not prevent him from pursuing numerous interests and constantly enriching his knowledge. If he had been born into more moderate circumstances, I postulated, Clark would have been both an exemplar slave dealer and an innovative slave breeder. Even as it was, he had enriched his estate considerably by frequently and astutely trading his own personal slaves and had certainly enriched my own estate by his sound advice in the complex field of contemporary slave breeding.

Just a few days after the funeral, the lawyers handling Clark Romney's estate visited me. Clark had no living relatives, they stated, and consequently had left half of his many properties to various charities and the other half to me. All his assets would be split according to the terms of his will once they had been appraised, including his home estate, his vacation retreat in Sicily, all of his investment portfolio of huge holdings in various business enterprises through the United States, his 14 estate maintenance and household slaves, his current pleasure slave, and – my birthday gift of years ago! They explained that Clark had never bothered to fill out the appropriate transfer of ownership papers for my birthday gift of the handsome black slave and consequently it legally had to be considered part of the estate and appropriately appraised.

"It's probably no surprise to you that all of Mr. Romney's properties were male," one of the lawyers felt it necessary to add. "Of course, male slaves generally sell at much higher prices than female slaves, so we're talking about more money in livestock than is true in most estates." That lawyer also mentioned that the 15 other slaves in Clark's estate were in their prime, were generally well built and very muscular and attractive, although not as strikingly handsome and well hung as his current pleasure slave of course.

"Normally, in a case like this," the other lawyer continued, "we take custody of the estate property you're currently holding, and place him in the pool of estate items to be auctioned off to settle the estate. However, since you have had the estate property under your roof for a number of years now, we could look at several other options. You could sign some papers acknowledging you have an estate property on loan to you temporarily and we could leave the slave here under your custody for now with payment of an appropriate rental fee so we don't look negligent as executioners of the estate; or we could arrange to have the slave appraised almost immediately and let you buy him outright from the estate at a non-auction 'fair market price' set by the appraiser; or, if you're tired of the property anyway, we can just take him with us now and add him to the estate holdings awaiting auction. The choice is entirely up to you, especially," he winked, "since half of everything will end up with you anyway. If you're tired of Mr. Romney's old gift to you, perhaps you'd like the temporary loan of some of his other estate slaves with appropriate rental fees of course until the estate is settled. Even the ones he bought to trim his gardens and hedges would make most satisfactory bed bucks I would think. I was expecting to find just some ordinary draft slaves but when I saw them the other day, I was astonished. Prime meat by anyone's standards – almost a waste to have them sweeping up and clipping hedges – especially at what he probably paid for them!"

"When you see the slave Clark gave me, you'll understand why I still have him," I laughed. "I suggest another alternative you have failed to mention so far. You let me keep my gift from Clark right here while you send an appraiser over and set a fair market price for him. Take that price out of my share of the estate, send me over the proper ownership papers on the property and forget about any rent payments. In return for any inconvenience this may cause you, why don't you and your colleague take a little break and enjoy the property under discussion while my cook fixes lunch for the three of us. He's in the front bedroom right now making up the bed and freshening the room. Just tell him he's part of the hospitality package today – he'll know exactly what that means – God knows he's entertained hundreds of my guests over the years now. I'll arrange to have lunch served in the main dining room around one o'clock. It's 11:30

now – that should give you sufficient time to enjoy and then freshen up – the slave can help you with that too in that there's a nice bath connected to the bedroom."

"You're assuming the slave will be appealing to us?" the lawyer cocked his eye. "I'm afraid I'm a little fussy when it comes to who I allow to pleasure me."

"He'll appeal to you," I stated flatly. "I've never found one living soul he didn't appeal to. Frankly, as your client, Clark Romney, himself used to point out, he's the sexiest piece of meat you've ever laid your eyes on, even though I know you've seen a lot of slaves over the years. I'm assuming, of course, that when it comes to slaves, you're not adverse to enjoying a male slave now and then – regardless of whatever your basic preferences might be in that area – at least – most people are at least that open in today's society."

"Yes," both lawyers muttered without going any further. The one lawyer then looked at his colleague who was already showing a bulge in his well-fitted trousers. Noting his colleague's obvious interest, he nodded agreement and without another word, both expensively suited attorneys headed up the main staircase for the front bedroom.

After ordering the lunch with my slave chef, I passed the front bedroom on my way to my office. Emanating from the room were the expected sounds: the black's familiar muffled groans as his ass was being plowed once again, some slurping sounds as the black slave was obviously simultaneously sucking off the other lawyer and the gasps and panting of men well into some serious fucking. Even from my office I heard some loud moans of men in the throes of orgasm including one memorable outburst: "Holy shit, that's the best fuck I've ever had," quickly adjoined by a deeper voice proclaiming, "By God, we've got to get something like this for ourselves."

Shortly after that, the whole routine seemed to start up again but eventually I heard slashing sounds which mean they were cleaning up for dinner. Promptly at 1 o'clock, both men appeared fresh as a daisy, remarkably relaxed, and, again, fastidiously dressed. Both had good appetites and the delicious meal was devoured rather quickly with considerable gusto. They certainly also appreciated the slave-chef serving the meal, my exceedingly handsome and very well hung slave from New York kept totally nude and fully body shaved. The slave also featured a tight brass genital clinch affixed around his large balls and admirable penis as well as both succulent tits pierced with shiny 2" brass rings, which highlighted his muscular pecs.

"Go ahead and fondle the slave if you want," I told the two lawyers as the dessert of small rum cakes was being served. "Nick appreciates the handling, especially if you would like some nice fresh slave cream topping your cake," I stated as I encircled the chef's huge organ and began to stroke it to a full erection. "I don't take cream with my cake, but a lot of my guests do and Nick here is always eager to accommodate them," as some pre-cum appeared on the chef's fully erect thick circumcised 10" shaft.

To my surprise, both lawyers took me up on my invitation and Nick had his balls fully drained before they had had their fill of the delicious rum cakes.

"Nick always fixes a delicious meal," I noted as Nick, now at least partially flaccid, cleared the dishes away swiftly with a big smile on his face from his master's compliment.

"I can see why you and Mr. Romney were such good friends," the up-to-now silent lawyer spoke. "You both seem to have an eye for the very best the markets have to offer," he commented viewing the firm undulating ass of the chef just leaving the room. "May I suggest you review Mr. Romney's estate slaves before we send them to auction? There may be some properties there you, as an obvious connoisseur of slave flesh, would want to buy yourself before we dispose of them. Some of them, if I may be so bold, rival even your magnificent chef in their appearance, although I doubt if they quite match the boy you so generously shared with us before dinner. That, Mr. Wiley (my family name), is a rare find indeed. I can see why you wouldn't entertain for a moment the idea of him being sent to market, no matter the small fortune he would undoubtedly bring there."

"Remember, Clark found the boy for me," I said, "so I imagine some of his other slaves around his estate might be interesting too. Yes, let me look them over before you ship them out, if it's no trouble."

"No trouble at all, Mr. Wiley. When would such a viewing be convenient for you?"

"Now," I answered much to their surprise. "I've got some free time right now and it sounds like fun. And please feel free to call me by my given name, Brent."

The two lawyers looked at each other, totally unprepared their invitation would be acted upon so quickly. Nevertheless, they both nodded in the affirmative, obviously unwilling to irritate me this early in the estate settlement, especially when their fees depended in large part on my satisfaction with their services.

Within a half hour, we were over at Clark's estate and the 15 properties were lined up. Clark's current pleasure slave, who I had fucked thoroughly many a time over the past few months, gave me a warm smile of recognition, happy to see someone he knew in the confusion of his master's untimely death.

Pointing to the one slave I was familiar with, I instructed the lawyers to make sure he was transferred to my ownership immediately. The pleasure slave fell to my feet kissing them among his tears.

"Thank you, master, thank you," he openly wept in happiness. "I didn't want to get sold again at market, master," he blurted out before catching himself, knowing he had spoken out without his owner's permission, a crime for any slave. "Sorry, master," he apologized as he silenced himself and again assumed the proper slave display position in front of me with his eyes to the ground in total submission to his new master.

"Another outburst like that, slave, and I will make sure you're sold off," I admonished the slave, "and to some old hag who's probably so desperate she'll fuck you to death in three months or some old fat man who is only interested in parading you around town by that big dick of yours without ever letting you get off," I laughed. "I know Master Clark used you pretty heavily and I intend to do the same but, like your former master, at least I'll let you unload now and then if you serve me well."

"Yes, master. Thank you, master," the slave responded, his tone reflecting both his sincerity and gratefulness for now having such a caring master. His tall neck collar forced his head into an upright position so his face could be viewed at all times, but his eyes remained rooted to my feet in front of him out of total respect and as a symbol of complete submission to his new owner.

The remaining 14 slaves were, as the lawyers had suggested, rather spectacular themselves. They were anything but the ordinary draft slaves one would expect for the type of work they did. All were between 18 and 24 years of age, all were very well hung, all had very muscular bodies without an ounce of fat on them, all shaved each other daily so there wasn't a hair on their body below their eyes, and all had been genitally banded exceptionally thickly so their large organs were very prominently displayed at all times. All had been fitted with the tall neck collars that forced their heads into chronic upright positions, which Clark always favored with his good-looking slaves. None had tit, nose, or ear rings in that maintenance slaves seldom did since such adornments might get caught in the tools they worked with. Outside of those commonalities, they varied in height from 5'3" to 6'6", had physiques ranging from lithe swimmer types to the muscle bound weight lifter types, were of every known hair and eye color, and were white, brown, black, and yellow in skin complexions. Everything from the gene pools of Scandinavia to the Middle East to Africa to the steeps of Russia to the jungles of India was represented, along with some Kansas farm boys, some swarthy New York Jews, some Polynesian beauties from Hawaii,, and even an exotic Chinaman from San Francisco, all bred in place or enslaved at one time or another before Clark purchased them. About 70% had been born into slavery; the other 30% were captives but with training so complete it was hard to tell the difference, almost perfectly representative of America's slave stock at that time.

From their demeanor, it was obvious all now totally accepted their slavery and knew they were slaves for life with the sole duty of pleasing whoever owned them. Some questioning of the displayed stock quickly ascertained that all had received special training in their sexual duties as part of their training regimen, all had been used by one master or another in that capacity since they had either been captured or come of age, and all expected nothing else from any new master. Within 10 minutes of inspecting them, it was obvious Clark Romney had acquired a literal harem of well-trained slave boys for his own diversion as well as to keep the place trim and tidy. Displayed in any setting, the collection would enhance any owner and certainly establish his expertise in picking out the best in male meat available in American markets nowadays.

"I'll take these other 14 too," I instructed the lawyers. "It will just save you the trouble of auctioning them off. Ship the ownership papers and the stock over to my estate this afternoon. Might as well put them to work right away rather them eating the estate's assets up sitting around in holding cages here. My steward will assign them their chores and their cages in my slave quarters after you turn them over to him. But have him bring their papers up to my office so I can get them filed away. I assume you'll have the transfers notarized and recorded properly?"

"Of course, Mr. Wiley – I'm sorry – Brent if you prefer. We'll handle all those details promptly. Do you want your new properties partially clothed for the transfer or will it be alright if we ship them over in the slave transport van exactly as Mr. Romney kept them here?"

"Clark always kept his slaves naked since they seldom left his estate. It will be the same at my place – I'm like Clark. I enjoy looking at them."

"Who wouldn't?" one of the lawyers smiled. "It would be a crime to cover them up in any way."

"I doubt if these slaves, with the bodies they've got, have had a stitch on for years now. Am I right, boys?" he boldly addressed the slaves directly.

"Yes, master," the slaves all broke into smiles and answered simultaneously. Indeed, most of the slaves thought, it was difficult to remember when they last weren't totally naked if you didn't count their tall collars and thick genital rings. The bred slaves among them had indeed never had clothes on in their life and the two or three captured slaves among them had certainly never had them on since first captured. Now all of them thought of their slave collars and genital bands as 'clothing' that distinguished them from non-slaves over and above their distinctive chronic nakedness.

By late that afternoon, I had fifteen more slaves at my disposal – another legacy of Clark. As my original gift from Clark, now actually owned by me legally, swallowed my entire length until my organ was suckled by his throat muscles as I idly played with his swollen erect tits, I reflected on how much my life had changed since I had first met my good friend Clark. Too bad he had met such an untimely death. Strangely, I felt cheated out of the Syrian slave he had taken with him in his death. Knowing Clark, I bet he was really something if he had traveled 50 miles out of his way to buy him. But then my back arched, my breath temporarily halted, and I shot a full and very satisfying load deep down my slave's throat directly into his stomach.

THREE MONTHS LATER:

Those two estate lawyers wanted one percent of my inheritance as their fees. I don't know about the charities that were getting the other half, but I thought it was outrageous and refused to pay since Clark's estate was sizable. I remembered how enamored they were with my handsome New York chef who had so graciously topped their rum cakes with his man-cream that afternoon several months earlier and offered ownership of him in lieu of their usual fees. Since I cleverly had the good looking slave right there in front of us sporting a huge erection while he was serving his famous rum cakes to my guests when I made the offer, they accepted my offer immediately and before I could find his papers to sign them over to the two lawyers, they had both milked him once again and were savoring the slave's cream atop their rum cakes as I rejoined them with the signed papers.

I wondered when was the last time they had accepted a milk stud in lieu of cash payment. But I knew my former chef was going to have his balls drained very regularly from now on, especially now that he had two masters to satisfy with his output, not just one. Besides, I was never into milking studs much so his only use in that area up to now was in pleasing my guests or showing him off for my friends. I knew from my breeding studs that regular draining of a slave's balls usually increases their production, so I was sure he would satisfy his two new masters given time. I had saved a lot of money by this trade compared to the fees they had in mind, but I didn't feel guilty about limiting the attorney's fees – the slave was a darn good chef and I would miss his talents in that area. I had the feeling the two lawyers could care less whether he could cook or not as long as he could steadfastly produce the sauce they liked so well.

CHAPTER 10

PRESTIGE COMES WITH AGE

TWELVE YEARS LATER:

After inheriting a sizeable hunk of my friend Clark's estate and the escalating profits from my slave breeding operation, which had been around long enough to see the crops annually reaching market age, I was now a very wealthy man.

Clark, in his infinite wisdom, had been right years ago about the future profitability of a well-run, selective slave breeding business that regularly produced predictable, high quality products that rivaled anything available anywhere. The 'Wiley' products, as they were referred to after my family name, consistently brought top market prices and they were indeed premium goods: about as well built as men got, almost indestructible in their disease-resistance and sturdiness, consistently strikingly good looking, and always very well hung with the sex organs well displayed since their bodies were always shaved totally smooth, their pricks were always circumcised, and all were fitted with thick genital bands. Furthermore, they were always eager to be used as indicated by their usual semi-erect dripping organs, always well trained as their subservient demeanor indicated in just a moment's observation, and totally accepting of their slave status. No purchaser ever had to worry about even a hint of rebellion or resistance to anything asked of the products. The 'Wiley' products were available in a variety of hues ranging from jet black to well-tanned blondes, and in sizes varying from small compact bodies that would fit into any bed to literal giants that could cover even the biggest broods of a rutting shed. Every owner preference could be accommodated among the multitude of bodies offered for sale each and every day – everything from a well-muscled but still delicate fresh-looking boy for an owner's bed to the huge, super-masculine studs in constant arousal that would be purchased to sire the next generation of slaves for the markets.

A separate branch of Wiley Industries offered female stock produced at the breeding farms. Most were bought, albeit at much reduced prices compared to the males, for assembly and manufacturing assignments, domestic duties, cleaning services, staffing the brothels catering to heterosexuals and lesbians, and, of course, the best among them as brood mares who were regularly mated with the highly selected studs to produce the never-ending crops of replacement slaves.

Not only was I busy running my various enterprises to steadily increase profits, managing my financial funds to give a maximum yield, and serving as a valued advisor to both corporate businesses as well as the U.S. Department of Commerce, but I was also frequently asked to give slave breeding and management lectures at numerous universities and corporate seminars in addition to serving as a contributing editor to two popular journals: SLAVE BREEDING and EFFECTIVE SLAVE MANAGEMENT. I had even, most recently, received the U.S. government's highest civilian honor: the "Distinguished Service Award" for my slave breeding innovations, specifically in developing a practical scheme whereas predictable strains of slaves best suited for particular work assignments would eventually evolve as a result of highly selective and carefully controlled slave breeding.

In others words, I was not only rich – I was famous or at least fast becoming so. It was hard to adjust to all the responsibilities and time demands fame placed on a person, but I set firm limits on my time, became immune to flattery and public acclaim, and deliberately made sure my personal life style was unaffected by all this. My main goal was, as always, similar to my late friend Clark's – enjoying life to the fullest, especially within the context of what owning others of the same species (more or less) could afford.

This meant I kept a whole stable of always ready and totally willing male slaves at my home – these were the very best of my own products and/or the best the markets had to offer all over the known world, regardless of cost. They were, without boasting, the best looking, well built, best equipped, best trained, best motivated, and the sexiest boys ever gathered in one place. Outside of skin color, they varied little from what I liked best in slaves: muscular well-built physiques featuring huge pectorals, rounded tight butts, tight abs, and colossal always-ready equipment. All were exceptionally handsome to my eye, and, catering to my own preferences, they ranged from cream colored to a shiny jet-black in skin hue.

Most important was their training: their overriding goal was to bring me pleasure with their bodies, no matter what was wanted, immediately and with grace. It didn't matter to me what their natural sexual preference was or whether they resented doing the acts asked for or not – they were judged on how well they met the demands, not what they 'thought' about doing them one way or the other. Therefore, I didn't have a bunch of very effeminate slaves around, yet alone those dressing or trying to act as female whores – I had real men doing what men did best to please another man. The fact they had no choice in the matter was incidental in that they were owned properties there to serve their master's needs, whatever they might be. All the slaves in my stable understood they were slaves first and foremost with no thoughts or feelings of their own that mattered other than how I evaluated them in performance of their duties.

No matter how hard they tried to hide it, it was obvious the majority of my stable slaves were naturally heterosexual given the choice, at least when I first acquired them. But they knew they didn't have a choice and adjusted accordingly to both their advantage and mine. After intensive training and a year or two of hard service, I would defy anyone to tell the naturally heterosexual from the naturally homosexual slaves. It was irrelevant unless they got sold off to a mistress for a change of pace, but again, adjustment to reality and their superb training would overcome any natural inclinations one way or the other.

My stable were all 'dressed' alike: totally nude, totally body shaved or with their body hair plucked out below the eyes, hair at least ear length with some shoulder length, 'tall' collared so their faces were always visible since they were forced to hold their heads upright at all times, tits ringed with moderate sized rings which made them erect and irritated them to eventually grow to two to three times their normal size over time, genitally ringed with thick bands which insured a full prominent display or their organs at all times, all trimmed (circumcised) so nothing was ever hidden from their master or mistress, small rings through their nose septum so I could leash them by their noses or hook them to a fucking bench easily, and most with one large ear ring in their left ear to offset the prominent ownership brand I had burnt into their right pectoral and left butt check. Many were fitted with semi-rigid plastic butt plugs when they weren't being cleaned out or getting fucked so that they typically walked with a little twist I found provocative. All were well fed and treated when sick although this was seldom enough. I ordered them to polish their teeth every day with a 'whitening tooth paste' to retain the beautiful teeth I required when I purchased them and cleanliness of their bodies at all times was mandatory along with immediate attention to any skin blemishes whatsoever. In other words, I spared no expenses on furnishing and maintaining them once I bought them. For what they cost to start with, it would be foolish not to. My 'stable' was my personal pride and joy and told me, more than anything else; I had made a success of my life. Each time I went up one of my slave's butts or thrust down their throats, I truly felt like a master – the feeling only obtained when you own the very best of your own species to do exactly as you desire, whether it's taking it up the butt, sucking you off, weeding your garden, cleaning out your toilet, cooking your food, making your bed, drinking your piss, or whatever turns you on. I used my 'stable' at least once a day and often more than that. Why not? They were mine and there for my enjoyment.

I had published two articles recently in the popular journals I mentioned. One lengthy one in SLAVE BREEDING outlined precisely the procedures necessary to produce a 'designer' slave line specifically bred to perform certain tasks better than others. It got heavily into the genetic contributions of the particular male stud and the specific female brood selected for breeding, the effects of the breeders' age, the time of breeding, the prenatal environment of the brood mare, the effects of diet and pharmaceuticals, the immediate post-birth environment, and the early specific training necessary for a successful final product. Of course, the heaviest emphasis was on the genetics of the male and female breeding stock and how these could be estimated prior to a subsequent pregnancy. In that article I predicted that ultimately slave breeders would have three distinct 'strains' of slaves available: heavy-duty but relatively stupid draft slaves best suited for most manual work; a more intelligent and slightly less muscular slave who required less food but who had great endurance for factory and small construction tasks demanded in great numbers by most corporations nowadays, and an extraordinarily handsome/beautiful slave with exaggerated sexual characteristics and drive best suited for domestic and leisure purposes as well as just for show who would be bright enough to intuit their owner's desires without too much prompting but certainly not bright enough to become philosophical or introspective, let alone reflect on their inherent inferior status as owned properties.

The shorter invited article in EFFECTIVE SLAVE MANAGEMENT mainly focused on exerting an owner's control of his property at all times. Thus there were recommendations for short rationing, types of food allowed, when to feed and water, the most effective disciplines within various types of slaves, e.g., use of the bullwhip and hot irons on draft slaves where permanent scarring isn't important; use of humiliation, shame, and embarrassment with the domestic slave; the balance between chronic hunger and quick response to a master's commands, the advantages of cutting vocal chords for certain types of slaves vs. the usual voice training; and the effective use of sexual rewards for slaves where all sexual outlet, when and where and how, is decided by the owner. Basic stuff, actually, but it never hurts to reiterate the obvious when it comes to slaves I argued. I also argued that while all slaves generally go naked when the weather is warm to save clothing costs, in colder climes the embarrassment of going naked when others are clothed can be maintained by fitting them with warm clothing that is at the same time humiliating – skin-tight clothes that emphasize their sexual organs; clothes that only slaves wear and are starkly different than free men's clothes; and the use of heavy nose rings to assure a 'slave look' regardless of what clothes they may have on to keep them from freezing to death. The article also addressed the proper use of women slaves in their dual role: as workers and as host bodies for the next generation of slaves.

I argued forcefully that women made excellent factory workers because repetitive tasks didn't wear them down as much as seemed to happen with easily bored men slaves and were actually better at fine detail work, especially in the making of jewelry and clothing. On both types of work assignments, women could be bred in a single afternoon and then chained back to their work post the very next day until at least two to three weeks before a scheduled delivery. Post-delivery, they could be back, chained to a familiar spot, within a week or two and bred again, often after just a few months time.

Male slaves, on the other hand, were not allowed to breed (with the exception of the highly selected studs who did nothing else), but their greater strength was best utilized in heavy assembly work and draft labor. Sexual release, under the direct control of their supervisor, and food and water intake, were the absolutely best motivators for male stock although I admitted that the whip, the tasers, and the huge disciplinary dildos found wherever you found slaves had their place in effective slave management. The easiest way to handle all this was to vasectomize them when all considerations for studding them had been eliminated, but this, of course still allowed their sexual drive to be used to your advantage.

I used as an example a factory-making slave transport vans where I had served as consultant. Female slaves did almost all of the assembly of wheels and the body van body itself and were usually chained to their work station where it was easy to discipline them if necessary with the usual scourges and rods. But I argued that threatening isolation from their fellow workers proved almost as effective as a good whip and was totally harmless to the growing pup within most female slaves who were profitably kept pregnant as much as possible in their dual role as worker and producer of slave pups. Food and water deprivation for female slaves was counterproductive when they were simultaneously being bred in that it would affect the precious new slave fetus within them.

Women slaves were social animals, I argued, and social rewards and punishments were by far the most effective and didn't threaten their potential as broods.

In contrast, big dildos, jammed well up a male slave's rear hole, were extremely effective in motivating and disciplining male workers. The dildo allowed the slave full mobility in his work space, gave the slave a constant feeling of being controlled in that he had the sensation of being fucked by a master's huge penis whenever he moved, and, dependent on their size, could be used for corrective punishment as well a motivational device. These large disciplinary dildos were huge – usually a good 10x6" so slaves fitted with them walked bull-legged at all times and squirmed uncomfortably at their workstations. Male slaves never seem to totally adjust to these types of dildos. They groaned as they were installed each morning before work. They groaned as they were removed for cleansing before scheduled for sleep, and they groaned as they had to torturously walk with the dildos embedded in them. In addition to rigid control of sexual outlets (which was the most effective reward outside of food and water), I strongly recommended all male slaves be fitted with dildos despite their cost – they were well worth it in the long run and, I argued, usually paid for themselves in increased productivity and total compliant behavior within just a few weeks. When training newly captured or sentenced slaves, the huge disciplinary dildos had shortened total training time a good two months after they were almost universally adopted in the training centers. Of course there, I pointed out; the only time they were removed was when a slave was either receiving his series of flushings or being fucked by one of the trainers. As everyone reading the article already knew, slaves in training rarely experienced not having something stretching their hole.

Both articles were well received and led to numerous speaking engagements where I could elaborate on the various points of the articles as well as answer specific questions. One of the most requested of these talks (and the one for which I received the highest speaking fees) was entitled: "When The Time Has Come: Replacement Costs vs. Maintenance." It tackled head on the question any slaveholder must face eventually – when does the cost of a replacement slave offset the lower productivity and higher medical costs of the aging slave? With slave prices steadily decreasing due to the increased output from the breeding farms, the wisdom of keeping slaves around past their prime no longer made sense. I argued four main points: (1) the older slave was often less productive, no matter how much you tore their hides to shreds trying to motivate them, and even that took up a lot of the slave handler's time and effort; (2) the medical costs involved in "fixing up" slaves often wasn't worth it – slaves suffering maladies and diseases were sometimes given expensive but often ineffectual treatments that cost more than a good replacement slave and you still ended up with next to nothing; (3) slaves' market value depreciates steadily with age so it often makes sense to get rid of them when they still bring at least sometime at the auction block; and (4) old slaves can still add to your profits – slaves terminated before disease makes their bodies worthless are now the main source of animal feed and fertilizer and salvage values are steadily increasing in this area. After I had the audience convinced it was time to re-evaluate their slave holdings with an eye to replacing those hurting the profit line, I offered a detailed scheme I had derived over the years to help make the final determination for each slave in a given owner's inventory. The equation included the purchase price of the slave, the slave's age, any diagnosed or suspected diseases, their gender, their main type of work (within broad categories), their food intake, and, for bred slaves, the longevity of their specific stud and brood mare. For captured or sentenced slaves, the scheme included age of enslavement, and the length of training required before the slave was tractable and totally cooperative. The regressive equation I promoted also had you plug in the current auction price of a potential replacement slave. With a few minutes of rather simple calculation, any owner could quickly figure out the cost advantage of replacement or retention.

Once this scheme was widely utilized, there was considerable more turnover in slave herds and, overall, productivity went up while maintenance costs went down. A nice side effect of wide use of this new decision-making tool was that the cost of animal feed and fertilizer took a dramatic drop. The feed specifically manufactured for slaves also suspiciously dropped in price over this same time, which everyone appreciated, but no one ever openly discussed. Slaves were one thing, but it was common knowledge the government inspectors out of Washington, D.C. had recently uncovered some "adulterated" sausage sold on the streets of Chicago itself. Some rumors had it the pork had been laced with some meat bought from some derelict slave dealers cleaning out their own pens, but others claimed the sausage makers were mixing in dead horsemeat purchased from nearby stockyards.

The Distinguished Service Award, primarily a result of the formulaic decision-making tool that was adapted by almost all large slaveholders throughout the United States, was the capstone of my career. It was presented at the White House by the President himself, was widely publicized throughout the nation by various government agencies concerned with the slave industry (Departments of Commerce, Treasury, and Interior as well as the National Chamber of Commerce), and certainly enhanced the value of Wiley Industries products by a good 10% price increase almost immediately. After the President's Award, I was swamped with all sorts of bids for my services where I could get into the details of slave breeding in a direct way.

The only offer I didn't decline was to have published a short illustrated manual on effective slave breeding. In that I went through all the usual time-tested procedures, but livened it up with actual sketches of selecting both male and female breeders, showing the actual breeding process so readers could visualize the best positions for maximum "hit rates," and details on how to cycle both the male studs and female broods to maximize successful impregnations. I used my old breeding stock as models for the artists illustrating this manual, including my own standbys – the original white stud and the helmeted black stud I had purchased later. Both were now well into their late thirties but still going strong and still looked like the amazing studs they were. It amazed even me how well they had held up both in retaining their youthful looks as well as their ability to always get a full erection and promptly deliver a full load of fertile fresh sperm four times a day seven days a week without fail.

By now, of course, their offspring was well over 10,000 each utilizing thousands and thousands of different broods, each brood on their hands and knees underneath the studs with their legs spread wide as the giant organs entered them and thrust away. I pointed out in my illustrated manual how the studs seldom saw the faces of those they were covering and consequently were unaware of whether they had covered that brood in some previous mating or not. It was made clear neither the broods or the studs ever saw their offspring. The slave pup was removed from the blindfolded brood immediately upon delivery and placed in a slave nursery where a rotating series of wet-nurse slaves actually fed and raised them through the first two years – a different one each day generally so no attachments were ever formed. The manual even gave a glimpse of how the slaves were raised in Spartan group homes without names or clothing outside of their slave collars where emphasis was placed at the earliest age on pleasing a future owner if they were lucky enough to get sold. The manual made clear that to the slave pup; the greatest peril in his life would be NOT finding an owner and simply being harvested as the group home wrote off its loss. The manual emphasized the importance of good record keeping throughout the entire process – from impregnation to final sale in that every buyer of the final product was entitled to a full provenance of each bred slave they bought.

The manual was a sensation when it was released by the booksellers and made me even richer. But all other offers I declined. My life was totally satisfactory as it was and I felt I was doing all I wanted to as it was. To do more would mean less time at the breeding operations making sure all was being done exactly as it was supposed to be done and by the right slaves at the rutting benches exactly as scheduled. It would mean less time spent with my 'stable' where I found my leisure taking on whole new heights of enjoyment.

My original gift slave that I had named "Slave," was still as good looking and sexy as ever thanks to a rigid forced exercise regime and a very controlled diet of only high-protein, high fat, slave food. That led to maintenance of a trim muscular body, a nice shiny black hide, and high sexual interest as evidenced by an almost constant, dripping erection even after all these years.

My original white stud was still pounding away at the rutting benches day after day, year after year and his "hit rate" remained as high as ever. He never complained at having to rut four times a day, seven days a week with a succession of women where he never even saw their face, he never seemed anything but pleased when I called him to my own bed on many an occasion where he was the one being fucked for a change whether it was up his ass or down his throat, he never seemed to get bored with the 'sport' of fucking as he called it, he never minded being observed studding in front of various audiences I would arrange, and he always seemed interested in maintaining his very high hit rate, always inquiring, when allowed to ask a question, as to how many he had 'knocked up' since the last time he asked.

The same was true with my only slightly younger always helmeted black stud, the second one I had purchased with Clark's advice. But the black stud, who couldn't speak or hear, did occasionally inquire in the primitive writing he had retained from before his accident, as to how many male pups he was producing relative to female pups (he seemed to take pride mainly in how many male pups he was producing), and, years later, he seemed interested in how much his progeny was selling for at auction. It was obvious he wanted to produce pups that brought his owner top money each and every time and took a personal pride in it.

Of course, as the business expanded, I had added whole cadres of new studs over the years, each as spectacular as the original ones, but some variation in the color of their hides and eye colors. The new studs modeled themselves after the old hands in this area, and unrelentingly almost strutted to the rutting benches with the sole intent of making another slave pup for their master's profit.

Not once did any stud ever voice a concern that he was producing thousands of new slaves just like himself under the total control of whoever had the money to pay for him. Broods did occasionally if you let them gab with each other very long and breeders always had to keep an eye on the broods to prevent a few of them from aborting their babies or sometimes, if not restrained properly, from strangling them with their bare hands when they had just birthed them. Seems like a few of them didn't want to produce slaves just like themselves who eventually would be bred like themselves to produce even more slaves, etc. But then, women can get sentimental if you let them and don't keep them busy enough to keep their noses out of their master's business. Men slaves rarely wandered off into issues outside of their immediate needs and making their life more comfortable by pleasing their master. Some women slaves got beyond themselves occasionally – what I called "philosophical" – a condition that should always be well within the master or mistress' province only. Only an owner had the 'big picture,' i.e., the information necessary to make appropriate judgments. Slaves had neither, the decision-making experience nor the long-range perspective an owner had. Every owner I ran into had experienced a few women slaves who thought, ridiculously, they could butt into this area. I recommended such women be transferred to close confinement in the mines where survival concerns outweighed everything else in their life. That usually brought an end to such nonsense and after just a few months there, any talk about what happened to the products of their body ceased once and for all. After all, their bodies belonged to the owner so they had no right to say anything about what their bodies produced. That too, of course, belonged to their master or mistress.

Other than the occasional lecture (which I limited more and more as I got older), my life was exactly where I wanted it. I had discovered, with my late friend Clark's help and advice, exactly how to build a huge fortune without excessive effort. I had done that with great alacrity and was now reaping the fruits of my success. Amassing great wealth was just a matter of mastering the basic fundamentals and then religiously sticking with them.

Clark had told me years and years ago, the money was in slaves and the greatest profits could be made in breeding them for market. How right he was. My only regret is he isn't with me now to enjoy my success. I knew up in the afterlife he was fucking that Syrian slave he took with him in that horrible car wreck or perhaps something even better by now. But still, I wished he could enjoy my stable – at lot of the slaves in it were just his type!

ABOUT THE AUTHOR

Bill Smith is a prolific author of well-regarded, well written, and widely read tales of homoerotic male slavery. Previous publications you may enjoy include: *BATES TRAINING CENTER, GUILIANO IMPORTS, THE FIRM, THE BRAZILIAN, THE MARKETPLACE,* and *THE PHYSICIAN*.

www.ingramcontent.com/pod-product-compliance
Lightning Source LLC
Chambersburg PA
CBHW070823250626
47170CB00006B/2199